Give M
Put It

Gretchen silently
sound of her dog's barks.

Instead of a wounded deer, Rocky was pulling at a sodden, mud-encrusted lump that lay half in and half out of the swamp. Years of nursing erased all sense of caution and Gretchen covered the remaining space in seconds.

It was a man. His face was turned to one side and bloodied. His skin was a dull gray-white. Gretchen immediately pressed her fingers to his neck, praying she'd find a pulse. To her relief there was a faint but steady throb.

He was alive.

JANET JOYCE

resides in Ohio and is happily married to the man who swept her off her feet as a college coed; she admits that her own romance is what prompted her writing career. She and her family like camping and traveling, and are avid fans of college football. Ms. Joyce is an accomplished pianist, enjoys composing her own lyrics and reads voraciously.

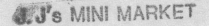

Dear Reader:

SILHOUETTE DESIRE is an exciting new line of contemporary romances from Silhouette Books. During the past year, many Silhouette readers have written in telling us what other types of stories they'd like to read from Silhouette, and we've kept these comments and suggestions in mind in developing SILHOUETTE DESIRE.

DESIREs feature all of the elements you like to see in a romance, plus a more sensual, provocative story. So if you want to experience all the excitement, passion and joy of falling in love, then SILHOUETTE DESIRE is for you.

For more details write to:

Jane Nicholls
Silhouette Books
PO Box 236
Thornton Road
Croydon
Surrey CR9 3RU

JANET JOYCE
Out Of The Shadows

Silhouette Desire

Originally Published by Silhouette Books
division of
Harlequin Enterprises Ltd.

*First published in Great Britain 1985
by Silhouette Books, 15–16 Brook's Mews, London W1A 1DR*

© Janet Bieber and Joyce Thies 1985

Silhouette, Silhouette Desire and Colophon are Trade Marks
of Harlequin Enterprises B.V.

ISBN 0 373 05199 9

22–1085

*Made and printed in Great Britain by
Richard Clay (The Chaucer Press) Ltd,
Bungay, Suffolk*

Other Silhouette Books by Janet Joyce

Silhouette Desire

Winter Lady
Man of the House
Man of Glory
Controlling Interest
Run to Gold
Rare Breed

For further information about
Silhouette Books please write to:

Jane Nicholls
Silhouette Books
PO Box 236
Thornton Road
Croydon
Surrey CR9 3RU

For our editor, Isabel Swift,
who fosters the creative spirit
by encouraging new and fresh ways
to express life's greatest pursuit—Romance.

1

Three men cradled their rifles and trudged across the field, heading toward a densely thicketed forest. The rising sun was just beginning to streak fingers of light across the horizon. Cornstalk stubble cast long shadows across the dark, loamy Ohio soil.

"This place doesn't look familiar," Tim Mosher remarked, resting his wiry frame against a fence post as he surveyed the upcoming line of trees. "Think you'll be able to keep us from getting lost this year, Hamilton?"

Michael Hamilton's blue eyes lost a bit of their normal good-humored sparkle. He grimaced, remembering last year's ill-fated excursion. After all his boasting about being a seasoned woodsman, he'd somehow managed to get them all lost. They'd spent hours wandering in an endless circle, and if they hadn't run across a local farmer, they'd probably still be roaming around in the forest. "Trust me, guys," he assured them confidently. "I brought a compass this time."

"You mean the old pathfinder is going to rely on more than his instincts?" teased Jerry Grimes, the oldest member of the trio, as he came up behind Michael. His tall burly form, clothed in a red-and-black checked jacket and pants contrasted garishly with the camouflage-print outfits worn by both his companions. Their only concessions to safety were the neon-orange caps perched on their heads.

"I'll ignore that," Michael said as he hoisted his gun to his shoulder and pushed the wire fence down with one hand. He waited until Jerry and Tim crossed over, then stepped over himself. They'd reached the edge of the woods and would soon be forced to remain completely silent if they expected any success.

"Cut down on the chatter, guys," Michael warned. "You know what happened two years ago. We lost the only good shot we had because we were laughing so hard over Tim's antler dance, we scared all the bucks away."

Jerry snorted loudly in his attempt to stifle a roar of laughter. "Hey, Tim. You bring your special doe perfume this year?"

"Naw, I learned my lesson. My wife wouldn't let me bring my coat in the house. Had to hang it in the garage for three months before that stink went away. She's beginning to wonder what we really do out here," Tim complained. "She's got a recipe for venison stew she's been waiting to try for years."

"This year she'll have her chance," Michael vowed staunchly.

Jerry gave Michael a crooked-toothed grin. He nodded toward the trees as he strode forward. "Come on, you slowpokes. You're walking these hills like old women. Get a move on or the deer'll be all done with their breakfasts and tucked in for a nap."

"We're not setting the pace, old man," Michael pointed out. "You're the one lugging a big beer belly."

Throughout yesterday's fifty-mile drive from Columbus to the forested center of the state, the three men had enjoyed their joking camaraderie. Although they were only acquaintances and otherwise had little in common, they did share a mutual interest in hunting and for a few days each year became buddies. Last night in their motel room, their hunting stories had reached wildly exaggerated proportions. Raucous laughter had accompanied their poker game, which had lasted far into the night.

They'd rousted themselves out of bed before the dawn, eager to start the day despite their brief hours of sleep. After a robust breakfast and several cups of strong coffee, their spirited gibing had begun anew. Now, however, it was time for hushed voices and a minimum of conversation.

The peace of the forest was broken by the distant tapping of a woodpecker and the rustling of the tops of the tall pines as they swayed in the wind. Leaves crackled and twigs broke beneath the men's booted feet as they tramped deeper and deeper into the forest. Michael let the tranquility of his natural surroundings seep into him, grateful for this four-day break. No assignments. No late-night assignations. No worry over what trouble his alter ego, Mack Dawson, might get into next. Nothing to do but relax.

As they neared the edge of a large clearing, Michael took the lead. He paused, listening for a betraying rustle in the tall reeds surrounding the swamp. Nothing. At least, not yet.

Michael gauged the wind. Carefully he skirted along the edge of the clearing until he judged they would be downwind from their quarry. This year they weren't going to alert the deer of their presence. This year they were going to reap the benefits of stealth, cunning, and superior intelligence and bag themselves a buck.

Michael smiled in self-satisfaction. Last week he had reread *The Last of the Mohicans* and felt a renewal of confidence in his pathfinding skills. Natty Bumppo, James Fenimore Cooper's legendary wilderness scout, had nothing on him. With the furtiveness of an Indian, he stepped silently into the clearing. He stalked to the edge of the murky water and bent his tall frame into a crouched position.

Hoping his companions would be suitably impressed with his skillful tracking, he studied the ground for hoofprints. The tracks were there, plenty of them. "Looks like a big buck's been by here," he said knowingly.

The deep swamp was an often used watering hole, but his two friends didn't need to know he'd learned of its location from the night clerk at their motel. "This is a good place to wait," he declared.

Next to the tracking, waiting was the best part of hunting. It wasn't the kill that Michael enjoyed. It was pitting his wits against the deer, enjoying the quiet sounds and scents of the forest. Even though he was a confirmed city-dweller, it was fun getting back to nature once in a while.

Pointing to the hoofprints in the soft mud, Michael looked over his shoulder at his companions. The grin that spread across his square-jawed face broadened.

Jerry and Tim were pointing their rifles directly at him. "Okay, guys. I get the message. I know I've led you over miles of hills this morning, but you don't have to get testy about it."

Michael's grin faded slightly at the sound of the first hammer being pulled back. "Empty your pockets," Jerry ordered.

Michael's brows closed together in an exasperated frown. "Come on, guys. You took most of my money last night. This isn't funny. Didn't the academy teach you not to point guns at people unless you plan to shoot them?"

"This is no joke, Hamilton," Jerry decreed, his grim expression and cold stare emphasizing the words. "Do it. Now!"

"My God!"

As Michael watched in stunned horror, Tim took aim. "Sorry, buddy," Tim apologized in a dull tone. "We've had some good times together. But now that we know you're Dawson, it's us or you."

Gretchen glanced up at the gray November sky and was reminded of a watercolor painting she'd done years ago in elementary school. The bare branches of the trees were like the black ink lines she had drawn on a paper washed with shades of blue and gray. She supposed her mother still had that painting neatly filed in a folder marked "Gretchen, Third Grade." After all, her mother had rarely thrown away anything produced by her only child. There'd been a place for everything and everything had been in its place within the well-ordered brick house where Gretchen Stockwell had grown up.

Breathing deeply of the fresh, forest scents, Gretchen

spread her arms wide and whirled around in a circle. Her hazel eyes shone with happiness as she pulled her wool stocking cap off of her head and tucked it in the back pocket of her jeans. Enjoying the feel of the brisk wind in her long hair, she lifted her face toward the sky.

As she filled her lungs with the cool clean air, her generous mouth widened in a smile. There was no hint of antiseptic, medicines, or city smog—nothing but the pungent odor of the earth, the sweet scent of dry leaves. She let out an exuberant whoop, a symbolic release of the constrictions that had compressed her for most of her twenty-eight years.

Honey-colored hair swirled around Gretchen's face as she twirled around in a small circle, then resumed her walk. Her booted feet trod soundlessly over the pine-needle cushioned ground as her long legs carried her deeper into the forest. Rocky, Gretchen's Great Dane, gamboled around her, barking happily as he responded to his mistress's excitement. "Feel it, fella?" Gretchen asked. "It's life, free and natural."

The big beast cocked his head and perked his floppy uncropped ears. His large, loose-jowled mouth hung slightly open and his tongue lolled out to one side. Gretchen giggled at the dog's comical expression, her laughter multiplying when the animal responded with heavy panting noises resembling breathy guffaws.

But for the rustling of the trees overhead, theirs were the only sounds. The forest lay dormant, settled into a long rest until the rich black earth warmed and everything would spring back to life once again. In the summer months nature flourished luxuriantly in what appeared a haphazard manner, its design coming solely from the hand of God. Nothing around Gretchen looked like the carefully manicured hedges and lawns that had surrounded her childhood home.

As Gretchen's feet carried her through the dense thickets that covered the rolling countryside, she knew what her conservative parents would think of her new home if they ever broke down and came for a visit. They would be appalled by the rustic log cabin, located in the middle of an untamed forest. It was nothing like the high-rise apartment they'd chosen for her when she'd completed her nurse's training. In the center of Columbus, Gretchen had lived in the secure, modern building for all of the six years she'd practiced nursing. She shuddered, not from the brisk wind that blew through the trees, but from the memories of those years that still haunted her.

She didn't like thinking about that time; the wounds were still too fresh. Instead Gretchen paused, swinging the large basket she carried, while studying the trees around her. Acorns. They were the reason she was out here, the main ingredient she required for her dye. Acorns created the particular shade of brown she envisioned for her next project, a wall hanging woven on the jack loom that occupied most of her cabin's living room.

Spying a large oak tree just beyond a stand of sumac, Gretchen started toward it. A mild snow flurry during the night had dusted the ground in patches, but she doubted she'd have much trouble finding the acorns that should be lying all around the base of the ancient tree. A bittersweet vine that had artfully entwined around the thick trunk and into the high branches was an added bonus. She'd collect some of the bright orange berries as well as harvest the acorns. Just before pushing through the sumac, she put two fingers in her mouth and blew a long, shrill whistle.

Rocky had loped far ahead of her and been gone for some time, but that wasn't unusual. The dog loved exploring the surrounding countryside, giving vent to the energy pent up in his strong, muscular body. Normally Gretchen wouldn't have worried, but deer hunting season was in full swing. Although she'd posted signs prohibiting hunting all over her property, Gretchen knew that they might have been overlooked, either innocently or purposefully. An excited hunter could easily mistake Rocky's size and coloring for that of a deer.

She whistled again, then listened for the sound of his large body crashing through the underbrush. Far off in the distance, she heard a deep, throaty baying, unmistakably Rocky's. He's putting up quite a roar, Gretchen thought, imagining Rocky's brindle-colored body dancing around a tree. Some brassy squirrel was probably scolding him from the safety of a high branch.

Gretchen's anxiety decreased. With the hubbub Rocky was making, she doubted any hunter would be nearby, for certainly the dog's racket would frighten the deer. It was no use whistling again. If Rocky had managed to tree some animal, he wouldn't come to Gretchen's whistle, no matter how often she repeated it.

Gretchen's basket was nearly filled when she realized Rocky's baying had taken on a definite pattern. Sometimes it was louder and insistent as if he had come closer, then the baying would drift farther away.

Moments later she could hear Rocky's whine between sharp, staccato barks. He'd never sounded so urgent before and it made Gretchen curious. "What's

16

the matter, fella?" she called as she pushed through the clutching vines and bushes in the direction of her dog.

"If you had a run-in with another skunk, you'll be sleeping in the shed!" she shouted as a terse warning. Crossing her fingers, she sniffed the air. Since she could detect no hint of "parfum de polecat," Gretchen quickened her pace. At least skunk was one thing that could be ruled out.

Unfortunately there was still the possibility that Rocky had cornered a raccoon who wasn't taking kindly to the dog's playful interest. If he was tangling with a coon, Gretchen prayed it wasn't rabid. Rocky had been innoculated, but still, a rabid animal could be vicious. Gretchen proceeded cautiously.

By this time Rocky's barks had given way to long, mournful howls, and Gretchen began to worry that he might be injured. She called out again and was relieved when Rocky came bounding through a stand of young pines. Burrs and nettles clung to his glossy coat but there was no evidence of injury.

Rocky pranced in a circle around her, then came to a stop, his large front paws planted wide, his long tail wagging wildly. A soft whine came from his throat and there was a definite look of pleading in his large eyes.

"Okay, big guy. Got something cowering up in a tree?" Gretchen inquired with humor, thinking how proud her gigantic but timid friend was when on rare occasions he'd managed to frighten another creature.

Rocky whirled around and disappeared through the pines. "All right, all right." Gretchen stared in the direction her pet had gone. "I suppose you want me to come see the evidence of your questionable prowess." Her smile disappeared when Rocky's spine-chilling howl split through the stillness of the forest. Something was definitely wrong.

On a dead run Gretchen took off through the pines. She scrambled down the hillside, clutching at sapling and prickly shrubbery to keep her footing. Remembering the salvo of shots she'd heard earlier that morning, Gretchen shuddered, having a premonition of what she might find when she reached her pet. Even though she knew the deer needed to be thinned out as much for the animals' survival as to minimize crop destruction, Gretchen hated deer hunting. Still more, she despised the hunters who didn't bother to track down an animal they had wounded, leaving it to die in helpless agony.

At the base of the hill Gretchen stopped. She saw her dog standing at the edge of the swamp. Walking slowly through the tall grasses, she prepared herself for the grisly scene she expected to find. Oh, God, give me the strength to put it out of its misery, she prayed as she proceeded.

Instead of a downed and wounded deer, Rocky was pulling at a sodden, mud-encrusted lump that lay half in and half out of the cold stagnant water. Years of training erased all sense of caution and Gretchen covered the remaining space in seconds. She fell to her knees beside the still figure.

It was a man, sprawled chest down in the mud at the swamp's edge. His face was bloodied, turned to one side. His skin was dull, grey-white. Gretchen immediately pressed her fingers to his neck, praying she'd find a pulse. To her relief, there was a faint but steady throb beneath her fingertips and she could hear his rumbly breathing. He was alive but unconscious.

A nasty gash ran along his temple and disappeared into his water-slicked hair. Since the wound had

18

stopped bleeding and the blood had congealed, her immediate concern was to raise his body temperature.

"We've got to get him all the way out of the water," she pronounced aloud as she rolled the man over onto his back.

She had to hurry. He could be suffering from both shock and hypothermia. She scrambled to her feet then bent over him, grasped beneath his arms, and tugged. Her feet slipped in the mud and she landed with a splat on her backside. She hadn't budged the unconscious man an inch.

Even though she was only five-feet-four, Gretchen considered herself to be fairly stong. Nevertheless, she wasn't much of a match for this man's dead weight. She judged him to be six feet or more and he probably outweighed her by at least ninety pounds. Determination and fear for his life started the adrenaline pumping and Gretchen tried again, planting her feet more firmly in the mucky ground. This time she was able to get him a little more out of the water.

"Come on, boy. Help me," she ordered her dog. "I'll never call you a dumb mutt again," she promised as the animal grasped the man's shirt in his great jaws and started tugging. "Come on, come on," she encouraged, over and over. Together, she and the dog managed to drag the man completely out of the water.

Gretchen allowed herself a few seconds to catch her breath, then went back to work. After checking for signs of broken bones and finding none, she shed her woolen poncho and placed it over the man's chest. She found it strange that he wasn't wearing a jacket in such cold weather, but she'd reserve judgment on that stupidity for later.

Rubbing his hands between hers, she studied his face

for any sign of consciousness returning. She checked his pulse again and was gratified that it seemed a trifle stronger. Was his color a little better or was that wishful thinking, she wondered as she rubbed his face, hoping to rouse him.

All the while Gretchen worked, she kept up a one-sided conversation. "You have to wake up, mister. Come on, you can do it. Open those eyes." On and on she pleaded until finally his thick, dark lashes fluttered open, then promptly closed again.

"Don't you dare!" she shouted, and prodded him in the shoulder. "Wake up! You have to wake up!" He moaned and Gretchen rubbed his cheeks again. "Come on. You can do it."

This time when he opened his eyes, they remained open. He stared glassily up at her. Gretchen was relieved to see that his pupils were the same size. "Get up! You have to get up," she ordered, and pulled on his arms.

"C–co . . . cold," he muttered, trying to curl into a fetal position.

Now was not the time for a gentle, patient bedside manner. "Help me!" she yelled, slapping his wrist. "If you don't get on your feet, you're going to die out here!"

She could sense the effort he was making to comply with her harsh command, and read the pain in his expression as he tried to raise up on one elbow. "That's it," she encouraged.

After several attempts she managed to help him stagger to his feet. As soon as he was upright Gretchen grabbed her poncho and settled it over his shoulders. Before he could crumple back to the ground, she slid her shoulder beneath one of his arms to steady him.

"Start walking!" Her loudly delivered order must have gotten through to him, because he began to move his feet.

"Rocky, bark. Talk to me, Rocky," she commanded her dog, hoping the animal's sharp sounds would reach the man and keep him from slipping back into total unconsciousness. Rocky complied and Gretchen continued her own brand of barking as slowly the odd trio started the long trek to her cabin.

"You've got to help, too, you big brute!" she cried as the man placed more and more of his considerable weight on her shoulders. "I can't leave you alone out here. It would take too long to go for help."

"C—can't," he mumbled through chattering teeth. "L—leave me alone."

"You've got to stay awake and keep moving!" she shouted, ignoring his groans of pain as she alternately pleaded and bullied him into action.

She lost track of time and her throat was aching and scratchy, but she managed to keep up her harangue as she half carried, half dragged him the distance to her cabin. Every time he stopped moving, she berated him, finding it was the only way to keep him going. Whenever her voice softened in sympathy, his step faltered and he tried to sink to the ground. She knew if she let that happen, she'd never get him back on his feet again.

Once, when her own strength gave out, she allowed them both to fall to their knees for a few moments before beginning again. "Get back on your feet! You can do it, you dumb lug. You can do it," she chanted. "We're almost there . . . almost there."

After what seemed like hours, days of struggling over the rough terrain, drawing on every ounce of strength she possessed to keep herself and the man upright, they finally reached her cabin. They fell through her back door onto the kitchen floor in a jumble of arms and legs. Gretchen lay panting and gasping, taking several minutes of well-deserved rest before slowly rolling away from the man and onto her feet.

Seeing that his feet were still dangling over the threshold, she took a deep breath. "Here we go again," she said irritably as she bent behind him, locked her arms around his chest, and dragged him across the floor.

That accomplished, she closed the door against the cold. Her jeans were damp and muddy and so were her boots. She stripped them off quickly and left them in a pile by the door.

Leaving her patient sprawled on the wood floor of her kitchen, she raced for her bedroom. Seconds later she returned with an armload of quilts, blankets, and towels. "The floor'll have to do. I just can't get you in any farther. It wouldn't have hurt you to skip a few meals along the way, you know." she informed him starchly, sure he couldn't hear her. His eyes were closed again, his breathing ragged and his body shaking.

Quickly and efficiently she pulled off his boots and layers of clothing, then rolled him onto the quilt. Briskly she toweled his large body dry before covering him with another quilt and heaping several blankets over him. Then she stepped over his swaddled body and went to the large iron cook stove at the back of the kitchen.

She opened the door, stirred the coals she'd banked earlier in the day, and fueled the low flames with the remaining split logs kept in a large graniteware pot. She left the loading door open on purpose hoping the heat radiating from the exposed fire would warm the room more quickly.

Bending over the man, she saw that his skin was no longer as gray and his lips had taken on a more natural color. "You look better already, but you need to see a doctor."

She straightened and stepped over him. Her telephone hung on a wall just inside the living room. To her dismay she discovered that the line was dead. From past experience she knew that phone outages were a frequent occurrence in the area. The system was locally run and much of the equipment was ancient. It seemed that a brisk wind, a heavy rain, or a layer of ice on the lines was all that was needed to interrupt service.

Coming back, she stood over her patient, hands on her hips. "I'll just have to bundle you up and take you to the emergency room."

Though his color was better, his skin was still too cool. Frowning, she sat back on her heels. "You should have a tetanus shot but I need to get you warmed up a bit more before taking you back out in the cold."

She had to keep stepping over the supine man in order to get back and forth across the kitchen which was no easy task, considering his size. Each time her long legs stretched over his head and wide shoulders, she landed barely beyond his head. She filled a teakettle and placed it on the range.

"You're even bigger than I thought," she grumbled softly as she stared in amazement at the unconscious man taking up most of the floor. "Whew! I don't know how I ever got you back here."

Rocky, who had placed his massive body alongside the man, lifted his head and gave Gretchen one of his lopsided grins. His wagging tail thumped enthusiastically against the varnished pine floor. "Yeah, you helped, too, old buddy. I guess we're a team," Gretchen

23

admitted with a grin of her own. "Stay snuggled up to him. Your body heat might help and I'll try not to think about all the mud you two are getting on my clean blankets."

Turning on the kitchen tap, she filled a pan with warm water and picked up a bar of soap. After pulling several cloths from one of the drawers, she recrossed the kitchen and went down on her knees beside the unconscious man. "I'm going to see what I can do about that wound while you're warming up. If nothing else, it needs to be cleaned, and the sooner the better." Gently she began washing his face. Once she'd wiped away the dirt, she saw a wide forehead, thick slanted brows, and broad cheekbones.

Even unconscious, it was a strong, very masculine face. Appealing, Gretchen thought fleetingly, as she soaped the man's square chin before concentrating on the angry wound at his temple. She dabbed lightly at it, glad to see that it wasn't too deep, frowning when she recognized the telltale residue of gunpowder.

"How did this happen, you poor, dumb fool?" she demanded even though she had a good guess. "Did you shoot yourself or did some other careless idiot shoot you?" His clothing had been so covered with mud and decayed swamp vegetation that it had been hard to identify, but she'd guessed it was typical of that worn by a hunter, except for the absence of a coat.

"Why weren't you dressed warmer? Are you so macho you can't make a concession to the weather?" she demanded exasperatedly as she parted his hair to get a better view of the shallow groove along the side of his head.

At least it looked like a good cleaning would be all the treatment necessary. That is, if he'd had a recent tetanus shot. If she applied some butterfly bandages to his temple, maybe he wouldn't need stitches. She stepped over him again and went for the supplies she required.

Returning to her patient, she was relieved to discover that his breathing was more normal and the tremors that had racked his frame had ceased. Using an antiseptic-soaked gauze pad, she cleansed the reddened streak that extended a few inches into the man's thick, curling dark hair.

"You're lucky you weren't hurt worse," she scolded when he winced in reaction to her ministrations. She tried to be gentle but knew the antiseptic stung.

After dressing his wound she checked his pulse again, this time aided by the second hand of her kitchen clock. "Not bad," she pronounced. "But you really should have your head examined. . . ." She giggled at her joke. "In more ways than one." She brushed her hand across his forehead, hoping his temperature was closer to normal, then tucked the quilts more snugly about him. "Anybody who hunts by himself has got to have a screw loose."

While waiting for the water to boil, she spent the time studying his features. He had an honest face. She'd found it appealing as soon as she'd wiped off the dirt and even more so now that is was relaxed, his color closer to pink. There was a boyish quality about it, though the dark growth of beard and the crinkling lines at the corners of his eyes indicated that it had been years since he'd been a boy.

His nose was straight with slightly flaring nostrils. His mouth, no longer tightened to a tight line against the cold, was wide, the lips firm and enticing. The slight indentations on each side of his mouth hinted at dimples. It was a mouth that looked as if it could cover a woman's lips very possessively.

"Good grief, I've been living alone in the woods too long," Gretchen admonished herself aloud. The man's unconscious, she thought—suffering from exposure and God knows what else, and I'm imagining what his kisses would be like.

His hair was still wet and muddy but curled in tight ringlets across his forehead. It was difficult to guess exactly what color it was, but she knew it would be quite dark, especially when she remembered the varying patterns of dark chestnut hair that were scattered over his body. When she'd been rubbing him dry, her thoughts had been strictly on the task at hand, but now in retrospect, images of his muscular body kindled her imagination.

He was somewhere in his mid-thirties—a man in his prime. His muscles were well-developed indicating that he took good care of his body. Gretchen reached for one of the towels and gently rubbed at his hair, hoping to get some of the swamp water out of it. As her fingers brushed through the damp locks on his head, springy curls wound around them. "It's not fair," she said, thinking of her own silky fine but stubbornly straight hair.

The teakettle shrilled its readiness and at the same moment the man opened his eyes, then squeezed them shut. His dark brows knitted together. "Shut that damned thing off," he grumbled tersely between clenched teeth.

2

Well, *hello* to you, too," Gretchen snapped. Two deep furrows developed between the man's brows and she immediately regretted her surliness. He was in pain. Springing to her feet, she stepped to the range and lifted the teakettle from the burner. The piercing shrill instantly died. Careful not to make much noise, she pulled a mug from a hook, dropped in a teabag and poured boiling water over it. After cooling the steaming tea with a little cold water from the tap, she returned to her patient.

"Here, drink this," she ordered softly, slipping her arm beneath his shoulders to lift him up.

"Head hurts," he mumbled, and resisted her efforts.

"I know but please try to drink this," she coaxed. "You need something warm in you." She scooted her bent legs beneath his shoulders.

In her single-minded concentration on getting the

man warm and dry, she'd completely forgotten her own state of undress. At the first contact of her bare thighs with the broad expanse of his naked back, she nearly leaped across the room. She was still clad in nothing but a loose cotton shirt and a pair of bikini panties!

Reminding herself that her patient was weak and needed her help, Gretchen tried to put her modesty aside. But it was difficult, because his dark head rested heavily upon the curve of her breasts and the moisture from his hair dampened her shirt. The cold wet contact seemingly erased the thin layer of fabric that separated them and Gretchen felt an immediate tightening in her nipples.

His damp head nestled against her breasts wasn't the only thing causing erotic sensations. The muscles in his back rippled against her thighs as he shifted restlessly. *He's just another patient.* Her short self-directed lecture didn't stifle her sexual awareness. *But I've never climbed onto a hospital bed half-naked with one before.*

To make matters worse she had to wrap one arm around his chest in order to support him. The sensation of the gentle rise of his pectoral muscles and the screening of curling dark hair brushing against her skin was so unnerving that her other hand shook as she raised the mug. Pressing the rim against his mouth, she forced a few drops of the tea past his lips.

He didn't resist any longer. After getting most of the tea down him, she carefully lowered him back to a prone position. She scrambled up to her feet, crossed the kitchen, and place the cup on the drainboard.

"Great legs."

"What!" Gretchen whirled to face him, her long hair swirling about her shoulders. She'd hoped to be dressed before he became fully conscious.

Michael Hamilton blinked his eyes but the vision didn't disappear. The woman was real, all soft curves and warm color. The silky fall of her honey-brown hair was haloed with gold by the thin ray of sun streaming through the window. Her eyes were wide, their hazel irises reflecting the tawny color of her hair.

Still, it was her smooth, feminine legs stretching upward from dainty, high-arched feet that kept drawing his attention. Every time he'd ventured to open one eye, he'd seen those shapely legs flying over his face. They weren't a figment of his jangled brain, not part of a dream—they belonged to this woman.

Where was he? Who was she? What the hell had happened to him? With agonizing slowness, he moved his head and took a good look around him. What kind of place was this, anyway? For a moment he thought he'd gone back in time to another century.

Hanging from the thick wooden beams of the ceiling were all kinds of things. Groups of candles were strung up by their wicks and clumps of dried weeds or some kind of dead flowers dangled from strings looped over nails.

The walls were made of logs and they were decorated with battered old pots and pans. An old-fashioned lantern hung from a hook by the back door. The sweet fragrance of burning wood permeated the air and heat flowed freely from the old Universal stove that took up most of the room.

How had he ended up on the floor of this primitive-looking kitchen, naked and suffering from the worst headache he'd ever had? Think! Think, Hamilton. Oh, God, now I remember. He shuddered in recollection.

For a moment Gretchen couldn't move, mesmerized by the man's intense gaze. Back at the swamp she'd been too concerned with his overall condition to register much about his eyes. They weren't dark and brown as she would have guessed, but slate gray—or were they blue? In the shadowed light it was hard to tell. Involuntarily she took a step forward. "How are you feeling?"

For a moment Gretchen wasn't sure he'd heard her question. His color was ghastly, a tense furrow grooved in his forehead, and his eyes were clouded. She couldn't be sure if he was struggling with acute pain or some equally intense and disturbing thought. She was relieved when his tormented expression slowly eased. A smile spread across his face, returning life to his eyes, eyes that were definitely blue, an arresting deep blue. She was again made very aware of her bare legs when those blue eyes began a slow journey from her ankles to her thighs.

"I must still be alive; angels wear much longer robes."

A hint of merriment appeared in his eyes when he saw her bare toes wiggling self-consciously against the cool floor. The dimples she had suspected were in his cheeks lit up his face as he took in her wet shirt and deep blush.

"Then again, maybe I did die." The words were deliberate as he concentrated on the smooth, almost round, face of his rescuer.

There's such an innocence and warmth about her, Michael thought. He should be able to trust her but . . . "If you're my angel"—he spoke slowly through an agony of pain that was renewed whenever he spoke—"I must have led a good life."

His voice wafted around her as disturbingly as his gaze, the raspy, graveled sound provoking every feminine nerve in her body. "You're very definitely alive, Mr. . . . ah . . . just who are you?"

"Right now I'm not too sure," he groaned in a thready whisper.

Gretchen edged casually—at least she hoped it looked casual—along the kitchen counter. She had to get past him, to her bedroom, and put on some dry clothes, but couldn't do that without again stepping right over his face. That had been all right when he was still unconscious, but it would be far too embarrassing now.

Why hadn't she pulled on a dry pair of jeans earlier when she'd had the chance? Now she was cornered in her kitchen. The wet material of her shirt was practically transparent, making it obvious to anyone but a blind man that her full breasts weren't supported by a bra. Self-consciously Gretchen crossed her arms over her chest in order to cover the jutting rose-hued nipples so vividly revealed. She desperately tried to think of a way out of this situation that would preserve some of her modesty.

As if he had read her mind, he murmured, "Am I holding you prisoner in your own kitchen or . . ." With difficulty Michael turned his head and eyed Rocky who was still snuggled close beside him.

The dog's massive head rested on his huge paws. His drooping eyes were fixed steadily on Michael, who glimpsed a row of large pointed teeth when the dog opened his jaw in the semblance of a yawn.

"Or is this beast *my* jailor?" he inquired warily. The gigantic dog looked capable of taking his face off with one bite.

"Rocky. Up, boy." Gretchen commanded, and the

Great Dane slowly rose, straddling the man with his huge paws. Gretchen suppressed a giggle when Rocky began to growl, a low threatening sound from deep in his throat. She knew it was Rocky's way of complaining. He didn't like deing disturbed from his comfortable position, but the man didn't know he had nothing to fear. Gretchen hid her smile at the man's decidedly worried expression.

"Bed. Go to your bed," Gretchen ordered sharply. The majestic dog gave his mistress a disgruntled look, then quietly ambled away, narrowly missing the man's face with one of his back feet.

Michael let out a long pent-up breath. He'd been afraid to move a single muscle. For a moment he'd thought his life was over when the beast had loomed over him, his huge jowls seemingly ready to close over his throat. "Does that dog bite?"

"Only when I tell him to," Gretchen lied, longingly eyeing the door. How much worse could it be to take one more quick leap over the man's head?

"You're not going to tell him to, are you?"

"Only if you give me cause," she answered absent-mindedly while she judged the distance of her jump. From where she stood she couldn't make it. She'd have to edge a little closer. Feeling the man's eyes on her, she looked down and noticed his expectant expression. "Did you say something?"

"I said I won't move till you tell me to. Please don't sic that beast on me. I'm in no shape to even fend off one of his fleas."

Keeping a straight face, Gretchen remarked, "I'll try to keep him under control."

If the man stayed long enough, he would discover Rocky was about as vicious as a newborn kitten, but in the meantime Gretchen welcomed this image of protection. After all, she didn't know a thing about this man, and although he was injured, he was huge.

Thoughts of her own safety hadn't occurred to her until he'd opened his eyes and raked her figure with such intimidating thoroughness. Once he'd gotten his strength back, he could . . . he could . . .

She'd assumed he was a hunter, but she didn't know that for sure. Even if he was, that was no measure of his character. For all she knew, hard-core criminals might like deer hunting. He had an honest-looking face, but then so had Baby Face Nelson.

Michael tried to raise his head, grimaced in pain, then laid it back down. "I suppose you want to get past me, but I think I'd black out if I stood up." With his eyes squeezed shut against the sharp throbbing, he asked, "Did you drag me out of the swamp all by yourself . . . ah . . . miss?"

"Stockwell. Gretchen Stockwell," she supplied hurriedly.

Keep your eyes closed, buddy, she begged silently as she sidled farther along the counter. She forced a calm tone. "Rocky helped me drag you out of the water. I got you on your feet and we walked back here. I could've used some help, but nobody else lives close enough to—"

She stopped dead in her tracks. *Dummy!* That was stupid. Now you've admitted you're here alone. If he makes one wrong move, you'll have to dredge up a due-any-minute husband.

Keeping her arms folded defensively across her breasts, she prepared to make her move. With one giant leap she could clear his head and be safely on her way to the bedroom.

Once again the man seemed to read her mind. All of her muscles were tensed for flight, but she was prevented from takeoff when a warm hand clamped around her ankle. "Don't do it."

"I was just going to get some dry clothes."

"You'll have to move me first. Every time you jump over my head like that, it makes me dizzy."

Every time? Had he been aware of her movements from the start? She almost died of embarrassment then, but there wasn't an ounce of male interest in his tone. Unless she wanted to make an issue of it, preserving her modesty was a lost cause. Besides, until he let go of her ankle, she wasn't going anyplace. "All right, I won't hop over you again."

His grip on her ankle eased and he removed his hand. Frowning down at him, she put her patient's needs before her own. It wasn't a good sign that her movement made him dizzy. "Are you having any trouble with your vision . . . ah . . . what should I call you? You never did tell me your name."

The man hesitated for an inordinately long time. Was he really having trouble remembering who he was? He wasn't suffering from amnesia, was he?

Michael Hamilton could think of no suitable response to her query. He couldn't give her his real name. Grimes and Mosher would probably come back to see if they'd really done the job. It was only sheer luck that they hadn't succeeded in their first attempt.

As the first rifle shot had been fired, Michael had taken a desperate dive into the water. Luckily, the bullet intended for his chest had missed, grazing his temple instead. He'd fought to retain consciousness against the pain and the stunning impact of the high-gauge cartridge while swimming underwater toward what he hoped was the opposite side of the swamp.

Even under water, he could hear the rifle shots and knew that Mosher and Grimes were firing into the swamp. Michael had remained under water until his lungs had felt as painful as the burning streak in his head. Fortunately, he'd surfaced beside a fallen tree. When his waterlogged jacket had threatened to pull him back under the cold stagnant water, he'd slid it off, trying not to make the slightest sound or ripple the water. He had heard Grimes and Mosher talking to each other as they'd poked around, firing several times into the concealing clumps of dead trees and tall marsh grasses.

"What d'ya think? Think we got him with the first shot?"

"Can't tell, but I think I hit him. Maybe he'll drown or freeze to death in this damned swamp."

"You're sure he didn't tell anyone where he was going?"

"Yeah. Said he didn't want to let on we're his contacts." There was a mirthless chuckle. "Guess this is the last contact he'll ever make."

"Better make sure, though. Clinton didn't pay us just to scare him. Gotta do the job right or the man'll send some of his boys after us."

"Too bad, though. I sorta liked him, even when he got all gung ho. Didn't ever expect to have to kill him."

"Yeah, well, you just remember it was a case of self-defense. Him or us. It'd only be a matter of time before you and me'd be on the wrong side of the bars."

As they'd drawn closer Michael had feared it was only a matter of time before they'd discover him clinging to the rotting tree trunk. It had seemed an act of providence when a third voice had sounded, identifying himself as a game warden. The man had been in the vicinity, heard the shots, and come to investigate. The warden had advised Grimes and Mosher that they were hunting illegally on private property, and unless they wanted a citation, they'd have to hunt somewhere else.

Michael had tried to call out to the warden from his hiding place, but the icy water and his wound had gathered their forces against him and he'd blacked out. The next thing he'd remembered was Gretchen's long legs streaking over his head and a blessed feeling of safety.

A chill of dread snaked down his spine. Prevented from finding his body, his assailants might come back and start searching for him again. He wasn't the only one with "pathfinder" skills. He didn't know how far Gretchen's cabin was from that swamp, but he doubted this little woman could've carried him very far. She reminded him of a plucky little partridge, long on tenacity but short on strength. How long would it be before his attackers came to this cabin and asked about him? What would she tell them if they showed up at her door?

"Mi . . . my name is Mack. Mack Dawson." Michael closed his eyes and turned his face away. He stifled a self-derisive groan. For God's sake, if he was going to use an alias, why did he choose that one? That was the name that had gotten him into all this trouble in the first place.

What if she had a copy of the *Columbus Sentinel*? If only his brain had been working faster he would have come up with something better. Telling her he was Mack

Dawson was just plain stupid. Even if she didn't recognize the name, Mosher and Grimes would and they'd be on him in a second.

Now he had more to worry about than his own safety—he had Gretchen's. This sweet-looking woman didn't have any idea what she'd gotten herself into when she'd rescued him. If they found him here with her, they'd kill both of them. He had to get out of here soon or he'd have to tell her the whole story. Would she believe him? Would anyone believe him? He was still having trouble believing it himself. Who was Clinton? He was sure he should know, but he couldn't place the name.

"Mack." It fits, Gretchen thought. He's as big as a semi. The name sounded sort of familiar, but she discounted it. If she'd ever met him, she was sure she would have remembered.

Gretchen crouched down beside him and held up two fingers. "Look at my fingers. How many do you see?"

"Uh . . . two." He had more to worry about than counting her fingers. Every hour might bring his assailants closer and yet until he was able to function, there wasn't a damned thing he could do about it. He was all but helpless. Maybe after a little more rest, I'll think of something, Michael decided. His brain just wasn't working yet. "How long have I been here?" he asked.

"Almost an hour. At least you're not having double vision, that's a good sign. We should be able to move you without much trouble. You've laid on this cold floor long enough," she informed him firmly. "I'll help you to the couch, then go get dressed. I'm taking you to the nearest hospital."

"No!" Hospitals reported gunshot wounds even if they were self-inflicted. He couldn't afford to let the authorities know his whereabouts.

Finally noticing the look of surprise that remained on Gretchen's face, he realized how suspicious his vehement denial must have sounded. "I mean," he stated more calmly, "if I can just rest a little, I'll be okay."

"But you should have X rays, a tetanus shot," Gretchen argued.

"Nothing broken. Just grazed me. Aim wasn't—"

"Somebody shot you?"

Fool! You've done it again, Michael thought. In another second you'll blurt out everything and scare this woman to death. He racked his beleagured brain, trying to think of a way out of the hole he'd just dug for himself. "No, no. Nothing like that. My aim . . . I mean . . . I dropped my gun and it went off."

It's time to take the bull by the horns, or rather the stranger by the shoulders, Gretchen decided. He was in no shape to make decisions, but she was. Any wound that had been soaked in fetid swamp water was reason for concern. "Okay, but you still need a tetanus shot. I'm taking you to the emergency room." With her most determined manner, she ignored his colossal size and stepped toward him.

"No," he protested feebly, his lower lip drooping in an amazingly childish pout. "Don't need a shot."

Gretchen's brows shot up in surprise. The man might be huge but he appeared to have the emotional responses of a five-year-old. "You sound like a little kid. Stop whining." Gretchen knelt down beside him and started pushing at his shoulders. "Come on, big boy. Let's get you up off the floor and onto the couch. You can rest while I get ready to take you to the hospital."

"No hospital. I don't need a tetanus shot," he insisted, mulishly. The slightest movement of his body set off a pile driver inside his head. "Leave me alone."

"It's only a little shot. It won't hurt much," she assured him, trying not to laugh. "You can take it." Ignoring his garbled protest Gretchen pushed at his back with the heels of her hands, then slid behind him to brace his body in an upright position.

"You can lean on me," Gretchen said, determined to get him to his feet. "We only have to go across the room. You might not remember, but we walked farther than that when you were in far worse shape."

"Oh, I remember," he drawled slowly. "You were merciless. Called me names and hit me. You might look like a harmless little partridge but you're a heartless bully."

Gretchen gasped. Partridge? She'd been embarrassed standing in front of him in panties and a wet shirt and all the while he'd been likening her to some plump little bird. Obviously he had no designs on her body. That should've eased her state of mind even more, but instead she felt insulted. She may have put on a few extra pounds lately, but she wasn't fat!

She was unnecessarily rough as she shoved against his back. "Get up."

"Take it easy, Attila," he complained, and leaned backward, taking deep breaths to ease the pain and dizziness.

His shoulders were heavy against her breast and his head rested on her shoulder, but worse his bare buttocks were now firmly wedged between her knees. If the sensations racing through her loins were any indication, his body temperature was up to normal, probably higher—or was it just hers that had shot up?

Taking a deep breath, hoping the intake of cooler air would help bring her back under control, she addressed herself to her task. She had to move fast and resorted to the kind of language that she'd found effective in dealing with him before. "Stand up, you big dumb lug!"

To her relief he meekly followed her command. She hid her smile as he slowly levered himself up with one arm. Gretchen added further support by slipping her arms around his waist. Gradually, he began to rise. The blankets slithered dangerously below his waist. Her arms were locked around his lean middle from behind and she feared what she might grab if she attempted to catch one of the blankets. Ordering him to move had been a big mistake!

Brazening it out, she forced herself to remain professionally aloof. "I'll guide you. If you're in pain, take deep breaths and blow it out through your mouth," she advised. "If you're dizzy from the movement, close your eyes."

But it was Gretchen's eyes that closed with her directions, even though she admonished herself for her prudishness. Being a nurse, she had seen scores of naked men, but for some reason she couldn't deal with this one objectively.

She moved to his side and balanced his weight with her shoulder. Hesitantly, she opened one eye. He'd grabbed hold of the quilt. Everything that was supposed to be private remained private. Thank goodness, she almost said aloud. With seeming nonchalance, she tucked the quilt around his waist and held it firmly there as she started him moving.

Careful not to jar his head any more than necessary, Gretchen guided him to the couch and let him lower himself to its upholstered surface. He lay there like a

40

giant mummy. Taking great gulps of air, he draped his blanketed legs over the edge, leaving his feet on the floor.

She grasped his ankles and gently swung his feet onto the armrest. Glancing up, she viewed his pain-whitened face with mixed emotions. She didn't like the sound of his breathing nor the pallor of his skin. She reached for the afghan and spread it over his chest.

Gretchen placed her palm on his forehead, alarmed to find it cool and clammy. "Mack?" she called softly. He stared at her, and for a moment she worried that he didn't remember her.

Mack would never let a mere flesh wound lay him so low, Michael chided himself. Get it together, Hamilton. Your survival may depend on it. He tried to adopt Mack Dawson's stoic behavior but succumbed to his own humanness and admitted, "God, my head feels like someone's inside it with a sledgehammer." His voice was rough, the words coming haltingly as if it were an effort to speak.

"I'm not surprised," Gretchen said sympathetically. "Your head's been creased by a bullet. At the very least you have a concussion. You've got to see a doctor."

"No!" he interrupted violently. "I mean," he began, his voice softer and more pleading. If Mack Dawson could get around women, then, by God, so could he. He'd done it enough times before. He offered his most beguiling smile, hoping his dimples were doing their job. "I told you before, that isn't necessary, Angel. I'm sure you've done everything a doctor would do. I trust you. I'll be fine, really."

It wasn't a lie, because now that he was lying prone again, Michael found that the pounding inside his head was beginning to subside. The room had stopped

41

spinning and he had no trouble focusing his eyes on the shapely woman before him.

Gretchen was very familiar with men who would avoid seeing a doctor until it was almost too late. Even though his smile came as a jolt, she refused to be affected by it. She knew every trick in the book and even that one wouldn't work. For the moment, she'd let him think she had given up, but as soon as she was dressed and ready, she'd bully "dimple cheeks" into the car. Maybe when that time came, she'd have help. "Is there someone I can call for you?" she asked solicitously.

Her soft melodic voice sent tremors through his body that weren't caused by pain or cold. "Huh?"

"I don't know how long you were out there but surely someone's worried about you. Have you a wife . . . family?"

She's genuinely concerned, he thought. I can probably trust her but . . . better wait, find out more about her. Besides the less she knows the less she'll have to lie about. But how do I know she won't squeal to the wrong people? *Squeal?* Jeezus, I'm even thinking like Mack. Watch it, Hamilton, you're turning schizo. Try to keep in mind what's fact and what's fiction. "No wife. There's nobody you need to call."

"Why did you go hunting all alone?" Her eyes narrowed, her expression revealing just what she thought of someone dumb enough to go out by themselves.

"You've already hit it—because I'm a big dumb lug." That was the truth. He'd been so stupid he hadn't figured out what was going on until he found himself staring down the wrong end of two loaded rifles.

Even good old Mack might have had trouble getting

out of that one, Michael thought with a wry grin. Bet Mack never would've thought of using the old reed trick, though. He chuckled with satisfaction, then frowned. Of course he would've. My thoughts are his thoughts.

The old reed trick hadn't worked very well anyway. Behind the branches of the old tree, he'd tried to submerge his whole body and breathe through a hollow weed but all he'd gotten was a mouthful of rank-tasting water. Funny how crazy you get when someone's trying to kill you. He'd wanted to curse Natty Bumppo and every other character he'd ever read about who'd managed to breathe through a hollow reed.

"Care to share the joke?"

"Oh . . . ah . . . no joke, except on myself," he replied vaguely, rapidly succumbing to a creeping exhaustion.

"Where do you come from, Mack?"

"Stop clucking, Partridge." He avoided her eyes. He supposed she had a right to ask questions, but for now he was unfit to field them. He regretted his harshness but couldn't think of another way to escape her penetrating gaze. He waved her away with one hand. "I'm going to sleep."

He nestled down in the cushions. Was that big thing with all the strings a loom? He must be hallucinating, because he could swear to God there was also a spinning wheel on the opposite side of the big stone fireplace. This whole day was beginning to seem like a segment out of *The Twilight Zone*.

He was ungodly tired, but most of all he needed time, time to figure out his next move. Maybe he should report what had happened, but considering who had just tried to kill him, he wasn't sure whom he could trust. He hadn't had this feeling since Nam, when even little children had been suspect.

"Of course." Gretchen sniffed, offended by his curtness. "I'll give you ten minutes, but then I'm waking you up and taking you in. Even if you don't think you need to see a doctor, I'm still not convinced."

She spun on her heel and headed for her bedroom, but after two steps flung back, "And you can stop calling me Partridge! My name is Gretchen." She'd rescued him, dragged his big, semiconscious body to shelter, tended his wound, and he had the brass to dismiss her without even a simple thank you.

"Gretchen."

She paused midway through the doorway but didn't turn around. What was the matter with her? The man was no doubt in a lot of pain, suffering from exposure and her feelings were hurt because he hadn't thanked her. He wasn't any different from dozens of patients she'd treated; he wasn't nearly as surly as some. Nurses didn't expect to be thanked for their work, but then she'd never taken care of anyone in her own home. Perhaps that was the difference. As his hostess she felt she deserved better treatment.

"Thanks for finding me and dragging me here." Mack's voice was thick with drowsiness. "I owe you my life." *I owe you my life! Sounds like a line from an old movie. I can almost smell the popcorn . . . or just the corn.* He would have laughed at his pun but was just too tired.

Instantly appeased, Gretchen turned back. Impish golden lights danced in her large eyes. "T'weren't nothin', stranger," she drawled seductively, then sauntered through the door.

The man on the couch felt his pulse rate increase as

he was treated to the view of perfectly rounded hips swinging beneath a shirttail that barely covered a delightful derrière. She might not like the name he'd given her, but it was certainly apt. She even twitched her cute little tail like a partridge. With a grin on his face, he drifted slowly into oblivion. Her breast was soft and full, warm and comforting. She was small and gentle, a bit feisty. . . .

3

~~~❦❦❦❦❦❦❦❦❦❦~~~

Gretchen threw the shuttle between the two rows of threads, pulled the beater sharply forward, then pressed her foot on the treadle. The shuttle, wound with rusty red yarn, flew back through the warp threads. Except for those times when she'd dutifully awakened the man on her couch, she'd been sitting before the large floor loom for hours, her hands and feet rhythmically guiding the warp and weft as the brightly patterned coverlet grew. The ancient craft she'd so recently mastered wasn't having its usual calming effect.

Biting her lower lip, Gretchen glanced at the man snoring on her couch, the man who was disrupting her hard-won peace. She found his presence far too stimulating, and that really bothered her. Until she'd found him, she hadn't thought much about her isolated lifestyle. For months she'd been perfectly content to be by herself, no responsibilities, no pressures, no involvements. Wasn't she?

She was at peace with herself and her surroundings. For the last few hours, however, she'd felt anything but peaceful. Although the sleeping man rarely moved, he seemed to be encroaching more and more on her private space, invading her intimate thoughts. Because of him, she was beginning to question her new mode of living. "Mack Dawson, this room ain't big enough for the both of us," she murmured under her breath.

Immediately thereafter, she recalled a similar statement she'd made to Mack hours before: "T'weren't nothin', stranger," she'd said, wiggling her hips. Why on earth had she done something like that? Because you wanted to show him that you weren't a dull, meek little bird, that's why! she answered herself. Trying to be honest, she also admitted that she'd wanted him to see her as an attractive woman, wanted him to be as affected by her presence as she was by his.

Gretchen Stockwell, if only your nurses could see you now. They'd never believe that Ms. Efficiency would intentionally flirt with a patient, let alone strut around in front of one wearing nothing but a damp shirt and panties.

She stopped weaving. Propping her elbows on the smooth wooden surface of the breast beam, she rested her chin in her hands. Ms. Efficiency. It seemed like forever since she'd been that person, and if she had anything to say about it, she'd never deserve that title again.

How proud she had been when she'd accepted her appointment as a charge nurse at St. Sebastian's. She'd applied for a job at the large inner-city hospital but hadn't expected to be placed in charge of an entire floor. Large and busy, 4C specialized in treatment of the acutely ill. The floor was always filled to capacity, receiving its patients through the emergency room and from the neighboring free clinics. For three long years Gretchen had ministered to the sick and dying of the ghetto.

She had started in her new capacity with true professional pride. Full of the idealism of youth, she had longed to ease the suffering of her fellow man, and she'd thought she'd be equal to the worst demands placed on her. As time passed, however, to keep from becoming an emotional wreck, she'd been forced to build a wall between herself and the dying. That wall had become thicker and thicker, until after several months she'd discovered that she'd insulated her emotions far too effectively. She'd rarely felt anything but utter exhaustion.

Moreover, she had realized that the very real human needs of her patients weren't being met. It wasn't enough to deal with just the physical needs of a patient, for in man, the psychological factors were as necessary to the healing process as all the intricate surgery, modern equipment, and sophisticated medicine available.

The whole patient had to be treated, but as the weeks and months had gone on, Gretchen had seen more and more evidence that this wasn't happening. There were many reasons. Shortages in staff, especially nurses, had worsened as the hospital's budget had continually been cut back. As charge nurse, no one had been more aware than she of the irritability that came with overwork, the personal frictions among the staff, and the extraordinary demands that had to be met in order to keep the unit running.

In addition to carrying a double load of patient duty, she and her nurses had been required to count and stack linens, sort infectious garbage, and move heavy furniture. When the unionized "transport workers" went off duty, nurses had to accompany patients in wheelchairs and on stretchers about the hospital. After the unionized housekeepers went home, it was the nurses' job to wipe up the floors and haul heavy supplies. If the electricians were off call, nurses were even expected to fix broken machines. They kept track of the floor's pharmacy, picked up after doctors, answered phones, counted narcotics, and picked up the meal trays and dirty linens—all without any increase in a pay scale that saw them earning less than the janitorial staff.

Misused as maids of all work, driven relentlessly to keep even minimal standards through their endless rounds of routine, many nurses on 4C found their commitment to nursing slowly eroding. Gretchen had felt it herself, and though she'd tried to rationalize her distant attitude toward her patients, she knew they had every right to expect some simple human kindness.

Exhaustion and frustration had been even more familiar to her than the nurses under her. Eventually she'd reached a point where her sensibilities were drained, her emotions were in turmoil, and a yearning for change had dominated every spare moment. The day one of her nurses had declared, "I can't be like you, Ms. Efficiency, I'm human," Gretchen had known she had to leave nursing. More than anything else, she'd wanted to get away to someplace where she could refresh her spirit and overcome her feelings of resentment and utter defeat.

Using her savings and a portion of a trust fund left to her by her grandmother, Gretchen had purchased this cabin and five acres of land in Hocking County, an undeveloped wooded section of Ohio. She'd hired someone to do the bulk of the renovation, then moved in as soon as the plumbing and electricity were completed. She'd undertaken the rest of the work herself, for the first time making herself a home that suited her tastes and personality, not those of her parents.

The physical labor had been therapeutic as well as money-saving, and now there wasn't a foot of space inside the cabin that didn't meet with her standards. It was a peaceful haven, her own private sanctuary from the frenetic pace of the outside world.

Glancing at the steeple clock gracing the mantel just beyond her loom, she saw that it was almost time to awaken Mack again. When she'd returned from her bedroom after throwing on a clean pair of jeans, a bra, and a shirt, Mack had been sound asleep. He'd successfully resisted any of her efforts to pry him off the couch and she'd finally given up.

It was only a temporary setback though. The need for a tetanus shot still bothered her, but she was willing to put it off for a few more hours. What she'd refused to give in on was awakening him at regular intervals and checking his pupils. Since they were consistently the same size, she had all but dismissed the possibility of a serious head injury. If he didn't complain of nausea, he was probably going to be fine.

"He must have a head as hard as a rock and with about as many brain cells," she remarked aloud as she reached for the beater and slammed it firmly against the weft she'd just thrown between the two rows of warp threads.

A rustling sound from the couch brought her abruptly out of her contemplations. She swiveled on her stool. "You're awake!" she exclaimed. The last time she'd looked, he'd been dead to the world.

"Yes, I believe I am," came the husky reply. Michael swung his feet to the floor and slowly sat up. Looking about the room a bit warily he asked, "Where's your dog?"

"Right over there." Gretchen's grin was teasing as she pointed to Rocky, who was curled up in the corner. "Why? You planning a wrong move?"

"Hardly," Michael said sheepishly. "I just feel better knowing where he is. I don't want him to sneak up on me."

He ran his palm across his chest then winnowed his fingers through his unruly mass of chestnut curls. "Would it be possible for me to take a bath or a shower? I feel like I'm covered with slimy things from that swamp you pulled me out of."

"Uh . . . sure," Gretchen managed. "I mean, you're welcome to use the bathroom—not that you're covered with slimy things."

All his natural color had returned. Evidently the man not only had a hard head but the constitution of an ox. He looked little the worse for wear except for the angry red streak, partially covered by the bandages at his temple.

Again, that wasn't all she noticed about him. She'd thought him good-looking when he'd been unconscious, a defenseless lump of masculinity. Standing upright with only the quilt draped loosely around his lean waist, he was a lot more than that. He was a beautifully well-developed man and downright sexy!

His curly hair was tousled over his forehead, his startling blue eyes still softened by sleep. The blanket opened to provide a display of one knee, a powerful calf and part of a hairy thigh. His muscled chest sported a thatch of curly dark hair that matched the curls on his head.

"The bathroom's right over there," she managed to say through dry lips. "You can go through either that door or the one in the bedroom. There are two doors."

"Two doors?"

"Yeah. It's an old cabin. I had the second bedroom turned into a bathroom and an extra door cut into it. I'll probably close up the doorway out here one of these days." Grateful that she had somewhere else to look, her eyes darted to the bathroom door. "There are plenty of towels in the cupboard next to the sink. Just help yourself to whatever you need."

He rubbed his jaw, the growth of whiskers making a rasping sound. "Does your hospitality extend to offering me the use of a razor? I must look like a bear."

"Yes—I mean, you can have a razor." Damnation! She'd done it again and the slow smile that crept across his face didn't help any. She got the impression he was very much aware of her discomfort and the reasons behind it. With as much composure as she could muster she added, "You'll find some disposable razors in the medicine cabinet above the sink. Is there anything else I can help you with?"

He took a few steps in Gretchen's direction, his blue eyes twinkling with a spark of mischief as he asked,

"Will you come to my aid if I faint in the shower or is that asking too much of your nursing responsibilities?"

The grin on his face made her doubt his need for any such aid. "I'll think about it if I hear a crash," she answered glibly, her tone and the narrowing of her eyes implying what she thought of his question. "I was a nurse for six years, Mr. Dawson. Dealing with only one patient is a piece of cake."

"What luck! My own private nurse. I hate to share," Michael said, then sauntered toward the bathroom.

She was amazed when he struck what she assumed was supposed to be an alluring pose, one hand draped over the top of the door. "After what we've been through together, you can feel free to call me Mack. It's much more friendly."

"We're not going to be together long enough to form a lasting friendship." She gave him a prodding gesture with her thumb. "Go take your shower, Mack, then we'll talk."

"Since you have nobody else to take care of, would you like to dry me off again?" He threw her another of his devilish grins. "You have such a soothing touch with a towel."

If Gretchen had had anything in her hands she would have thrown it at him. How long had he been conscious before she'd known about it? Had he really been aware of her rubbing his naked body dry with a towel?

Things were going from bad to worse. It was hard enough dealing with the knowledge that he'd witnessed her ungainly leaps across his head, but now it appeared he'd even been aware of her activities earlier on. She tried to remember if she'd done anything he could interpret as indecent. Of course she hadn't! Her thoughts hadn't been completely innocent, but her behavior had been above reproach.

A moment before the door clicked shut, he teased again, "And you do have great legs, Nurse Partridge. All the way up."

The man had a rakish streak a mile long and irresistible dimples to match. She'd wanted him to notice her, so now that he had why should she be so upset? Because he was far too engaging and she could easily lose her head, that's why!

Before she'd recovered from his last statement, the bathroom door opened and Mack's head reappeared around it, his dimples flashing.

"What else do you need?" She sighed in mock exasperation.

"I was wondering if you had any clothes I might wear. I seem to have lost mine somewhere."

"They were wet and covered with slimy muck. I threw them in the washer while you were asleep. You can have them as soon as they're dry."

"Thank you, Partridge. You *are* a gem." The bathroom door closed again.

Gretchen could hear the sound of the shower and got an immediate picture of Mack's nude body standing beneath the warm spray. In her mind she could see him lathering soap across his broad, hairy chest, down his muscular belly, and beyond. A flush of warmth spread from her stomach to her toes. She jumped up from her stool and began to pace the breadth of the living room.

What *was* this fascination she had with this man's body? The male form hadn't held any mystery for her since her earliest days in nurse's training. She'd dealt with hundreds of male patients, bathed them and seen to their most intimate needs. Not once in all those times had she ever felt anything like this.

She desired Mack Dawson, a complete stranger! It'd been a long time since she'd had this feeling, not since she'd thought herself in love with an intern whose good-looks and flirtatious manner had enticed her right down his primrose path. That relationship had come to a painful end as soon as she'd overheard him with another nursing student, using the exact words he'd used so successfully on Gretchen.

After that, hurt but far wiser, she'd made it a point to steer clear of any involvements with med students and, later, licensed physicians. Unfortunately, in her line of work, those were almost the only men she came in contact with, so her social life had become nearly nonexistant. There had been the occasional blind date arranged with someone's friend or relative and she'd attended some parties in her apartment building, but no one had sparked her interest beyond a second date. She wasn't soured on men, it was just that if given the choice between going out with someone she didn't care about or staying home with a good book, she'd choose the book every time.

She continued her pacing until she noticed Rocky watching her from the safety of his bed in the corner. His soulful black eyes were reproachful. "I suppose you like him," she accused, her tone camouflaging the unpalatable thought that she might like him too, and far too much. She was instantly answered in what she interpreted as the affirmative. Rocky's tail thumped enthusiastically against his bed.

"You would! You men always stick together! But just because he arrived here as wet and bedraggled as you did, doesn't mean I can adopt him too!" Even though that was an intriguing thought. Now you're being totally ridiculous, she chided herself. You can't take in a stray man like you would a stray dog.

Rocky had worshipped the ground she'd walked on from the very first moment, but Mack Dawson was a totally different proposition. He might appeal to all of her senses, but she hadn't seen much indication that the reverse was true. He'd flirted with her, but she wasn't so naive that she took it seriously. Although she could enjoy a harmless bit of fantasy, imagining Mack as a helpless stray starved for her affection, if it ever went beyond that, she might really regret it.

Thinking over her situation she had to laugh. She'd left the city because she was tired of schedules, of a controlled if hectic environment. Well, no one could say her life was predictable now. A year ago, who could have predicted she would have taken in a stray dog, especially a big lummox like Rocky? Now, six months later, she had taken in a big lummox of a man. But she wasn't taking him in, she reminded herself. The man was here for only a few hours—absolutely no longer!

She considered Rocky a refugee like herself. She had surmised that someone from the city had dumped him out in the country because their cute little puppy had grown much larger than they had expected. She'd named him Rocky because he'd overcome so many odds to become the healthy, muscular beast he was now. Besides, his large, drooping eyes had reminded her of Sylvester Stallone.

She contemplated the name she'd give to the second stray she'd picked up in the course of a year. Dimple Cheeks had a body that resembled Stallone's, but his eyes were more like Paul Newman's, blue, piercing, and sparkling with mischief. His dimples were as deep as Shirley Temple's but didn't connote innocence. On the contrary, Mack Dawson was no Rebecca of Sunnybrook Farm.

Her dark scowl prompted Rocky's soft whine. "Don't look so sad. I won't turn him out until he's more recovered."

If she didn't know better, she'd have thought the dog nodded his head in approval. He ambled to the door and scratched the floor, his sign that he needed to go out. She opened the back door. "Don't be gone long. I'd like to have you around when that man gets out of the shower."

Moments later a buzzer sounded. Gretchen walked to the dryer, yanked open the door, and started pulling out the contents, most of which were Mack's clothing. As she sorted and folded the garments into a neat stack, her thoughts took a far more serious turn. Why hadn't there been anything in Mack's pockets?

It was odd, she thought, remembering how her father's pockets had been absolute treasure troves of miscellanea, objects that gave clues to his identity and habits, objects that were deemed necessities. Necessities like keys, keys to houses or apartments and to vehicles. Maybe Mack's wallet, keys, and whatever else men carried in their pockets had been lost in the swamp.

Hell-fire and damnation, she stormed inwardly as she gathered up Mack's clothing. After I get him to the hospital I'll probably have to stick around and drive him to . . . where? She had no idea where he lived, where he'd come from.

Thinking back on when she'd found him, she couldn't even recall seeing a gun. Surely she would have noticed it. If he'd shot himself, shouldn't his gun have been lying close by? She supposed he could have dragged it in with him when he'd fallen into the swamp, but the more she thought about it, the more suspicious she became. How many accidental self-inflicted wounds were to the head? Hunters usually shot themselves in the legs, feet, even the chest.

And there was the lack of a jacket . . . even a hunter with rocks for brains would have worn a hunting coat of some kind. A coat would not only provide warmth against the cold November weather but also had large pockets to hold ammunition, pocket knives, and lots of things. It didn't make sense. None of it. Not the location of the wound, not the hunting alone, and most of all not the empty pockets.

As Gretchen continued pondering her guest's supposed accident, Michael was trying to clear his brain by lingering in the shower. Here he was, Michael Hamilton, mild-mannered reporter for the *Columbus Sentinel,* living out the fiction he'd created, a victim of his own overactive imagination.

He'd been a mystery buff since he'd seen his first Alfred Hitchcock movie. For years he'd nurtured a dream of writing one himself. When he'd submitted a proposal for a serialized mystery, he'd been delighted when it was accepted for print.

The story, "Bikinis, Rackets, and Smack, taken from the case files of Mack Dawson, Private Eye," had begun running in the paper over a month ago. If Michael had known then what he knew now, he would have thought twice about publishing that particular story.

As a news reporter, he'd covered several drug busts, and though Mack Dawson's case was a work of fiction, Michael had used information he had discovered about the actual drug traffic that existed in the area. He had hoped to entertain his readers and also increase public awareness of the seriousness of the local problem.

Hard-nosed, ruthless, womanizing Mack Dawson had begun to unravel the case of a tri-state drug ring operating behind the legitimate front of a tennis club. Mack was getting very close to discovering the identity of "Mr. Big," but Michael hadn't realized how close he'd been getting to a real-life kingpin.

God! Never once had he suspected that the police involvement he had created in his story was no fiction. Jerry Grimes and Tim Mosher were two of the finest cops on the force, or so Michael had thought before they'd tried to kill him. They were even on the narcotics squad. Now what was he supposed to do? Who in the hell could he trust? He had no idea how widespread this thing had gotten. To be on the safe side, he couldn't even contact the local police. He had it on good authority that there were regular marijuana drops in the area. It was possible that Grimes and Mosher had chosen the location because they had no fear of intervention.

Barney? Maybe he could call Barney Shultz. He worked for the F.B.I. Even though they'd bowled in the same league for years, Michael couldn't recall exactly what Barney did in his job. Was he an agent? With his rotund body and bald pate, Shultz hardly looked like one but maybe Barney could put him in touch with the right people. And maybe Barney'd know who this Clinton was that Mosher and Grimes had talked about.

A stab of self-pitying anger pulsed through him. This should never have happened. His identity as the author of the Mack Dawson series was supposed to be a well-kept secret, known to only a handful of people at the newspaper. Part of the promotional hype before the series had started had been about the mysterious author who didn't want to be identified. That meant whoever had informed Grimes and Mosher must be an employee of the paper. Was someone at the *Sentinel* involved in the drug ring? Was it his editor, Ed McDowell?

His first thought had been to call Ed, but then he'd remembered that McDowell had wanted to scratch the story because of its concentration on the illegal drug industry. McDowell had worried over libel and it had been the owner, Geoffrey Van Neff, who had finally sanctioned the series. Van Neff had encouraged Michael to write his series as realistically as possible.

Michael recalled how vocal Van Neff had been in his criticism of the local authorities. According to Van Neff, the police force wasn't moving on this criminal action and maybe a little public pressure could be brought to bear. Though the work was fiction, Van Neff had recognized there was enough truth in it to make people think. Hoping to inspire public interest, Van Neff had personally directed the publicity that had heralded the Mack Dawson series.

All Michael and Van Neff had wanted to do was stir things up a little. "We stirred things up, all right," Michael muttered bitterly.

He turned off the tap, wincing at the sharp pain that shot through his head when he shook the water out of his hair. "Fine time for you to go to the Bahamas, boss," he grumbled. His bad humor wasn't helped when he was forced to wrestle with the circular shower curtain that enclosed the ancient clawfoot tub. "Let me out of here," he demanded, shadow boxing with the plastic drape and the grasping fronds of a huge fern as he searched for the exit.

After winning the bout, he stepped out onto a pink fluffy thing he took for a rug and looked around for a towel. Gretchen had told him to look in the cupboard. He was half-afraid to pull on the delicate looking glass knobs of the rickety cabinet that leaned into the corner for support. Covered with goose flesh, he tested a door. It came open easily but inside he found nothing but shampoo, soap, and various cleaning supplies. Disgusted, he gingerly tried the other door and found a stack of pastel linens. "You call this a towel, Partridge?" he complained. "It barely covers my ass."

Standing in her bedroom, Gretchen heard his disgruntled remark. The connecting door to the bathroom was slightly ajar. She had no intention of answering him.

The delightful aroma of soap and steam filled her nostrils. She could hear Mack moving around inside and imagined him standing before her vanity, shaving that dark beard from his square chin. One of the towels he was complaining about was probably hitched hazardously around his lean hips, or was he standing there wearing nothing at all?

Damn him, anyway! Why couldn't he have at least kept the door closed? Remembering the size and ventilation in that room, she immediately answered her own question. Steam would have filled the space, making it impossible to see the mirror unless he'd cracked open the door. All she needed was more torture. She had enough trouble thinking of him covered with slimy swamp water, let alone contending with thoughts of his clean damp body, fresh from a shower.

Taking a deep breath, she grabbed the sweater she'd come for and rushed toward the door. Her burst of speed was immediately halted when the bathroom door came open. She bounced into the solid wood, then backward onto the footboard of her bed. Losing her balance, she flailed at the air as she toppled over onto the mattress.

A burst of deep laughter had her clambering off the bed. Mack's tall, broad-shouldered figure filled the bathroom doorway. "You're not hurt, are you?" It didn't look as if he was greatly concerned, for his dimples were like deep craters and his lips trembled with suppressed laughter.

"Huh-uh," she mumbled dumbly. Just as she'd imagined, one of her feminine bath towels hung precariously on his lean hips. She would stay immune to his charming dimples, sparkling eyes and gorgeous body if it killed her. "It's not that funny, Dimple Cheeks," she snapped.

"I'm not laughing at you but at that." He pointed to her rustic four-poster as another fit of laughter overtook him.

The bed was fashioned from tree trunks and topped with a canopy made from twisted twigs. The lop-sided heart-shaped headboard was woven from grapevines. It really looked like it belonged in a treehouse rather than a cabin, but Gretchen had seen the design in a magazine and fallen instantly in love with it. She'd built it herself and although it didn't exactly match the picture, she was quite proud of it.

Defensively, she said, "This is a perfectly wonderful bed. It's . . . it's a—"

"It's . . . it's . . . a nest!" Hearty laughter interrupted

his speech. "Perfect for a partridge." More chuckles. "You . . . build it . . . yourself?"

"Yes, I did," she said very deliberately, enunciating each word. "I'll go get your clothes. If you're through insulting my furnishings, you can get dressed so I can take you to the hospital. Maybe you won't find the accommodations there so hilarious!" Furious, she pushed him aside and stormed into her living room.

He was right behind her. Keeping the corners of his towel together with one hand, he reached for her. Instead of her shoulder, he got a handful of long tawny silk.

Gretchen felt as if her hair were being pulled out by the roots. "What are you doing?" she yelped, and twisted her head. Michael let go of her hair but several strands had become tangled in his fingers and he couldn't remove his hand without hurting her even more.

"Get your hands out of my hair!"

"Hold still. I'm trying."

Gretchen was too angry to listen. She twirled around and the motion carried his arm with it. A second later they were standing face to face and he was staring down into her mutinous, golden-hazel eyes.

A stunned look came over his face as the pink towel slithered to the floor. "Don't look now, Partridge," he teased. Every inch of his damp nakedness was pressed against her soft body. "But I've lost my fine feathers."

She was already aware of that fact and didn't dare move. She could feel the warmth of him, could see nothing but a mass of curly chest hair, and if she looked down . . . well, she wouldn't.

"What'll we do now?" She swallowed hard and

squeezed her eyes shut. Not looking didn't help. She could still smell his clean skin, feel the heat of his body along every inch of her front. Her hands hung limply at her sides. It was all she could do to keep from running her palms along the hard, male flanks just beyond her fingertips.

"Oh, hell," Michael groaned, struggling with his conscience. He knew damned well what Mack Dawson would do in this situation. Of course, it would have worked out better for Mack. The woman would have been the one minus her towel.

His fingers were tangled in her hair and he hadn't the slightest desire to remove them. What he wanted to do was pull back her head and kiss her. He'd been wanting to do that since he'd first laid eyes on her. He might not be as cocksure or as aggressive as Mack, but he recognized a heaven-sent opportunity.

With steady pressure, he pulled on her hair. "I'm human, Partridge, and you're delectable."

4

Gretchen opened her mouth on a startled squeak but the sound was muted by a pair of very masculine lips. Mack's mouth *did* cover a woman's very well. She was invaded by the rough texture of his probing tongue, the hard pressure of his lips. She tasted mint and Mack Dawson, a tantalizing flavor that made her hunger for more. She felt like she was soaring, flying away from the real world, weightless in the heavens. Needing something to hold on to, she flailed for support, her hands grasping the nearest solid object. A pair of bare buttocks, firm and warm.

At the feel of Gretchen's fingers digging into him, Michael moaned and lifted her softness against the want of his loins. She was so small, so soft . . . so female. She tasted like she looked, warm and sweet, like golden honey. Her heart was fluttering like a captured bird's against his chest and more than anything he wanted to cage that feeling within his own heart.

Gretchen became aware of how far things had gotten out of control when she felt his hard thigh nudge between her legs. The pressure of his unfettered masculinity against her thigh was doing alarming things to her, and if they didn't stop soon, she was going to succumb to the wild longings building up in her.

She pulled back her head, forcing an end to their embrace. She hadn't really been soaring. He'd lifted her feet right off the floor and she hadn't realized it until she tried to push away from him.

Inadvertantly, her swinging feet kicked him in the shin. He let her go abruptly and what followed was a humiliating experience neither one of them was likely to forget for some time. Getting his fingers untangled from her hair, rescuing the fallen towel, and recovering from an overwhelming attack of desire all at the same time proved impossible. When they were finally separated, Gretchen wasn't the only one wearing a bright red blush, but at least she was wearing something else.

Her gaily embroidered Western shirt and heavy jeans hid the rosey hue that covered her entire body. Michael wasn't so fortunate. He had nothing to veil his body's powerful reactions.

If Gretchen hadn't been so flustered herself, she would've laughed as he let loose with a string of obscenities and marched in naked glory to the bedroom. The last glimpse she had of him was the matched set of tight male buns disappearing behind the door.

"We can either go through all this again," he bellowed through the wood, "or you can throw me my clothes!"

Gretchen's expression became speculative. She

weighed her alternatives. She finally had him at a disadvantage and would be a fool not to act on it. "I'll give you your clothes," she crooned in a singsong voice, "if you promise to go to the hospital and get a shot in that cute . . . oops."

"Dammit, Partridge," he yelled back angrily. "I had a tetanus shot two months ago and I don't need a doctor. The pain I'm suffering at the moment isn't in the head. Press your luck and I'll come out there and prove it."

Breathing heavily, Michael leaned back against the door. Now that was a Mack Dawson line if he'd ever heard one. Maybe he should write it down and use it in a future segment. Mack was never intimidated by a woman. Michael Hamilton, on the other hand, wouldn't return to the living room for a million bucks. He'd been upfront enough for one day.

There was a knock on the door. He stepped aside as it opened, and he gave a sigh of relief when his clothes came sailing through. He took their appearance as a sign that Gretchen had bowed to his wishes. The next thing he'd have to do was persuade her to let him spend the night.

Charm. Turn on the Mack Dawson charm. If that doesn't work, you'll have to resort to Michael Hamilton's feigned helplessness. What nurse could resist that? A woman who looked that soft wouldn't put him out in the night, would she?

He had to make some plans, contact Barney. For the moment Gretchen's cabin seemed a relatively safe place. He doubted anyone would try looking for him tonight, but he'd be on guard just in case. They'd probably wait until tomorrow morning. By that time he hoped to be gone, but where? He couldn't go back to his motel, his apartment, the newspaper office. He was sure those places were already staked out.

No, he wasn't going anyplace until he'd called in some reinforcements. If the partridge didn't cooperate, he'd have to get tough. That's what Mack would do.

One step at a time, Hamilton, he thought as he buttoned up his flannel shirt, tucked it into his fatigue pants, and planned his next move. "I'll protect you, little Partridge, while I figure a way out of this. If I'm lucky you'll never have to know what's going on."

He eyed the unique bed one more time, not able to keep from grinning. Such a perfect place for his little partridge to roost each night, he thought, then wondered if she ever shared it. What would it be like to nestle down beside Gretchen's soft body beneath that canopy of twigs? Remembering how she'd returned his kiss and the feel of her in his arms answered his question. She was a warm, generous woman, holding a lot of passion inside her small body.

Putting aside that pleasant thought, he stepped cautiously into the living room, looking for the massive beast Gretchen called Rocky. Not seeing him curled up in the corner, Michael proceeded toward the sounds in the kitchen, hoping nothing he did would annoy the dog. Stepping through the doorway, he spied Gretchen but no dog and assumed, with a great measure of relief, that the animal was outside.

Gretchen had done some heavy thinking of her own while he'd been dressing. No man who could flirt and kiss the way Mack did was in any need of medical attention. His being here was doing wild things to her thinking. If he stuck around much longer, her libido would take over, and she had too much respect for herself to let that happen. From that kiss she knew he'd be a very satisfying lover, but there had to be more involved than physical gratification for her to share her body.

"Okay, let's go," Gretchen said as soon as he appeared, proud of herself for overcoming her desire in favor of her self-respect. She stood at the back door, impatiently jangling her car keys.

Michael ignored her command and sat down at the small drop-leaf table just inside the kitchen area. He dazzled her with a winning smile that was accompanied by a negative shake of his head. "I thought we agreed I didn't need a doctor."

"You convinced me of that, Dimple Cheeks, so you can stop grinning from ear to ear. Since the phone's still out and you can't call anyone to come get you, I thought I'd take you back to wherever you came from. I'd take you to your car, but you seem to have lost your keys and everything else you might have had in your pockets. Your car won't do you much good unless you were dumb enough to leave it unlocked."

Well, charm obviously wasn't having any effect, Michael thought wryly. He shifted a bit uncomfortably in his chair. He hadn't thought about his lack of wallet, keys, or anything until now. That must have seemed very strange to her, but he was certain he could give a feasible explanation. "Everything must have fallen out of my pockets when I fell in the swamp."

He schooled his features into a pleading expression, praying she'd respond to helplessness. Getting around this woman was no easy task. "I have nowhere to go," he mourned piteously. "I can't remember where my car is or anything else about the morning."

He continued giving what he hoped was a bewildered, lost look. He remembered very well where his car was—parked safely in his apartment building's garage. Mosher had insisted on renting a van for the trip, a very nondescript van. "Can't I stay here with you? Please."

"Oh, come off it!" Gretchen exploded, losing all patience. "There's no way you can pass yourself off as a homeless waif. You're much too well fed." Armoring herself against the pleading blue eyes that were beginning to remind her of Rocky's, she plunged on. "Do you live around here?"

"No. Eh . . ." he hesitated. *Think fast, Hamilton. If you tell her you're from Columbus, she's liable to drive you there; it's not that far away. Your apartment is the last place you want to go.* "I'm from Chicago," he blurted.

"Chicago!" Gretchen spluttered incredulously. "Then, what on earth are you doing around here? No one in his right mind would drive four hundred miles to go deer hunting by himself!"

Dig yourself a bigger hole, Hamilton. You're not very good at this thinking fast on your feet stuff. It was getting more and more difficult to come up with credible answers. *How true those words were—What a tangled web we weave . . .*

"What were you doing out there?" Gretchen probed.

It was obvious to Michael that the plucky partridge wasn't buying much of his story. *That's it for charm and helplessness,* he decided. He was left with two choices. Fess up or intimidate the hell out of her.

Since he didn't want her involved, he chose the later. He'd continue spinning out the lies until he could get out of her life. *Get tough and stall,* he ordered himself. *Stall until you can get through to Barney. If only the damned phone were working,* he'd call to-

70

night and get the hell out of here while the getting was good.

"That's none of your business, Partridge." His features became a cold, intent mask.

"I'm sorry if you thought I was prying." She quickly changed the subject back to the matter of his spending the night. "Staying here is out of the question."

Her statement fostered a frigid glare. "I would rather have had your permission, but now I'm telling you. I'm not going anyplace tonight. Whether you like it or not, you're stuck with me until morning."

Gretchen was amazed at this sudden change in him, not only amazed but intimidated. What had happened to the entincingly slashing dimples and beguiling smile? Then again, why should she be surprised at anything he did? The man was a shameless manipulator. This was probably just another one of his persuasive tactics. He wasn't really someone she should be scared of . . . or should she?

Not for the first time, she questioned the circumstances that had led to his head wound. He was lying to her about that, she just knew it, and that made her nervous. The man could be dangerous.

Chicago? Maybe he really was from Chicago. Weren't there lots of thugs in Chicago or was that only in the movies? Maybe there was a contract out on him. What better place to bump off somebody than a swamp in the middle of a remote area? His body might not have been found for days, weeks, months . . . maybe years. She bit her lip to stifle her growing unease.

She knew what would happen to a body left in a swamp, and the thought made her nauseous. For God's sake, Gretchen, get a hold on yourself. Your imagination's going crazy.

"You must've had a motel or a room in one of the lodges. I'll be happy to take you there," she babbled nervously. "I'm sure you'd be more comfortable. I've only got the one bedroom. You'd have a working phone. You could call . . . whomever."

From the look on Gretchen's face, Michael felt as if he'd just grown a pair of horns. The poor little bird was chattering nonstop. Maybe he'd come on a little too strong. "Calm down. You look like you think I'm an escaped convict or something. Believe me, you don't have to be scared of me. I'll let you go in the morning."

Let her go? Escaped convict? Is that what he was? My God! Gretchen thought with growing horror. Let her go in the morning? Was she his hostage? The Chillicothe Correctional Institution was just down the road. That would explain everything. That's why he had no identification. He'd been wounded in his own escape. Oh, Lord, what kind of crimes was he guilty of?

The man sitting at her kitchen table giving her a cold-eyed stare might be desperate. No telling what he could do if pressured. I'd better humor him, she decided. It might be my only chance.

Trying to appear nonchalant, she hung her poncho back up on a peg by the door. "I'm not scared," she lied. "But I sure am hungry." She hoped he didn't notice the trembling in her legs as she walked across the room. "How about you?"

Not waiting for an answer, she flew to the refrigerator. Searching desperately through the contents, she spied the remains of the casserole she'd made the day before. There was plenty left for the two of them, and all she'd have to do was heat it up. She'd feed him. He wouldn't bite the hand that fed him, would he? Or was that only dogs? How did she know what this kind of person would do? Speaking of dogs, where was Rocky? Just when she needed his questionable protection, he'd decided to go out and explore the county.

Michael had to cover his mouth with his hand to hide his grin when Gretchen nearly dropped the foil-covered dish before she got it to the oven. I'm better at this Mack Dawson stuff than I ever dreamed, he thought smugly. "Food's a good idea. I'm starving too."

But when Michael saw how badly her hands were trembling, his joy at being successful with his tough-guy routine quickly fled and was replaced by a strong wave of guilt. He'd really scared her. It wasn't fair to keep her in complete ignorance, but if she was this scared now, how would she feel knowing somebody was out there trying to kill him and might kill her too?

He'd never had to worry about anybody else before, and he didn't quite know how to handle it. It was a strange feeling, completely foreign to his nature. She was a responsibility he couldn't afford at the moment, but he was very reluctant to let go of her now that he'd found her. To his surprise he discovered that he enjoyed being taken care of, liked the feel of her in his arms. The way she called him Dimple Cheeks made him laugh and he liked that too. In fact, there was very little about her that didn't appeal to him on some level or another. He even respected her for not being entirely susceptible to his brand of charm.

Maybe it was true that danger heightened all your senses. He certainly was very much aware of Gretchen Stockwell as a woman. Her delightfully rounded derrière, full breasts, and sweet face were difficult to ignore. However, it was the sensitivity, the vulnerability in her soft hazel eyes that called out to everything male in him.

Fear for his life was fast becoming a secondary concern. As idiotic as it might seem, what was foremost in his mind now was how to get Gretchen to let him share that nest of a bed. If he did that he'd be taking his Mack Dawson fantasy one giant step farther, and the thought was almost irresistible.

Mack wouldn't think twice about tumbling any woman into bed, but Michael Hamilton? He didn't think he could rationalize using Gretchen's soft body, then walking away—perhaps forever. He might not have cared about anybody but himself before, but he couldn't remember having consciously used anyone either, especially a woman. He was already guilty of enough with Gretchen, and he wouldn't add more to it

A delicious aroma mixed with the fragrant wood scent from the stove, and Michael's mouth began to water. He hadn't eaten anything since five o'clock that morning, and his stomach reminded him of that fact by rumbling loudly. "Whatever that is, it smells wonderful," he complimented politely. He'd hoped his words would soothe Gretchen, but at the sound of his voice she dropped the knife she was using to chop apples at a cutting board.

"It . . . ah . . . it's sweet shepherd's pie." Gretchen retrieved the knife, rinsed it off, and nervously resumed her chopping. After scraping the bits of apple into a dish, she added raisins and a can of pineapple. Then she tossed the mixture and placed it on the table.

There was a loud scraping at the door and Gretchen all but flew across the room to let Rocky in. The big animal bounded into the kitchen, came to a halt in front of Mack, and sat down. If it hadn't been for the friendly thumping of Rocky's tail upon the floor, Gretchen might have been able to continue the charade that Rocky was a vicious protector who had taken up a sentinel post. Now only an absolute fool could misinterpret Rocky's behavior. The beast was all but begging to be scratched behind the ears.

Gretchen would've been heartened if she'd known that the man sitting at her table with an outward facade of calm was anything but. The brindled Dane that had parked his large body inches away from him was giving Michael considerable discomfort. The animal's tail was wagging. Wasn't that a sign of friendliness or would the beast rip his arm off if he tried to pet him? Tentatively Michael extended his hand, letting the dog sniff him, ready to snatch it away at the first sign that the animal was preparing to close his massive jaws over it.

To his surprise and extreme relief, Rocky slipped his broad, black-striped head under Michael's hand. "Why, you're nothing but a big phony," Michael pronounced, and scratched behind the velvety ears, thinking to himself that it was something they had in common. "Is he always like this or am I just lucky?" he asked the woman cowering beside the counter.

"I'm afraid so," Gretchen admitted, begrudgingly. There was no use keeping up the ruse. Rocky had laid his head across Mack's knees and before long would be practically crawling into his lap. Of course, she might be able to salvage some of the deception. "He'll be your friend as long as you're no threat to me. Then"—she paused for affect—"I don't know what he'd do."

It wasn't a lie. Rocky had never been put to the test. There was always the chance he might attempt to protect her . . . growl, step between herself and an assailant, maybe even attack. She hoped Mack didn't remember that Rocky had continued sleeping peacefully in the corner while Mack had gotten his hand caught in her hair and hadn't even twitched an ear during what followed. Of course, neither she nor Mack had had the dog on their minds at that moment.

"Gretchen, I promise, I'm no threat to you." Michael continued fondling the dog's ears but with ever growing guilt. He, personally, was no threat to Gretchen. Hurting her was the farthest thing from his mind. Making love to her was closer to the point. However, his mere presence in her home posed a threat. He prayed that phone service would be restored quickly. Barney Shultz was his only hope.

Gretchen brought the steaming dish from the oven. "What would you like to drink?" she inquired as she pulled glasses and plates from the cupboard.

"You wouldn't happen to have any bourbon or Scotch would you?" After all he'd been through, Michael felt the need for something more fortifying than the weak tea she'd forced down him earlier.

"I think you need food far more than a drink," Gretchen snapped without thinking. Then, remembering that she didn't want to anger this man, she amended hastily, "I mean, your body's been through a lot today and—"

"Exactly." He jumped at the opening she'd given. "That's why I'd like a drink if you have any."

She had a full bottle of bourbon stashed away in the back of a cupboard, but she didn't want the man drinking much of it on an empty stomach. What if he drank too much? No telling what kind of a drunk he was, and there was his head injury to think of. She didn't want to bring up that argument again, so she tried bargaining. "If I let you have one drink, will you eat all your dinner?"

"Lady, right now, I'd make a bargain with the devil

himself for a glass of anything alcoholic." Seeing her hesitation, he added, "I'll be a good boy and eat everything on my plate. Scout's honor." He held up his hand and made the Boy Scout signal.

Giving in, Gretchen rummaged in the cupboard beside the sink. She found the amber-colored bottle and brought it out of hiding. "Okay, just one. But if you don't hold up your end of the bargain, I'll sic Rocky on you."

"Please, not that," Michael pleaded with mock horror. "He might lick me to death."

"Probably would," Gretchen muttered, hoping her chagrin didn't show as she poured bourbon into a glass. "Do you want some ice and water with this?"

"No, thank you. Straight is fine."

With the first gulp of the potent liquid, Michael felt renewed. He relished the burning sensation of the undiluted whiskey as it streamed down his throat and into his stomach. "Ah," he remarked with satisfaction. "Exactly what I needed." He drained the contents and held up his glass. "Could I have a refill?"

Gretchen heaped shepherd's pie onto a plate and placed it in front of her dinner guest. "Nope. You promised to eat your dinner first." She handed him his silverware. "Now, eat!"

"How about another one after dinner?" Michael haggled, deliberately wielding his dimples. "You could call it dessert."

"I'll think about it." She sat down, spread a napkin on her lap, and dished up some of the casserole for herself.

Temporarily appeased, Michael addressed himself to the gigantic portion of some green and orange concoction she'd placed before him. He wasn't used to eating anything he couldn't get from a fast-food restaurant or heat up in a foil-covered tray. It was disconcerting to introduce food into his mouth that he couldn't identify, but he was hungry enough to eat anything. It smelled pretty good, so he was willing to give it a try. Besides, he reminded himself, you're a guest in her home—an unwelcome guest.

He shoveled a large forkful of the casserole into his mouth. Startled by the unexpected flavor of the mixture, he almost gagged. "What's in this?" he demanded, reaching for his glass of bourbon, finding it empty, and grabbing for the glass of milk she'd insisted on furnishing.

"All sorts of things. Broccoli, spinach, a little onion, green pepper, carrots, tomatoes, and—"

"Sweet potatoes!" he ejaculated. He drained his glass of milk. "Isn't there any meat in this mess?"

"Nope," Gretchen answered between bites. "It's completely meatless. Americans eat too much meat as it is. There's everything you need in this meal." She pushed the bowl of apples, pineapple, and raisins toward him. "Don't forget to have some salad. Remember, we made a deal and I held up my end."

"That was before I knew you were going to poison me with sweet potatoes."

"A deal's a deal. Besides, I believe your exact words were that it smelled wonderful."

"Smells can be deceiving and I was starving."

"So you said. Eat up."

The meal continued in silence except for Michael's repeated requests for more milk to wash down the all-vegetable dish. When he was done he placed his fork neatly on the middle of his plate and remarked, "That wasn't too bad after I got used to it. The apple stuff was pretty good."

"What are you doing, trying to butter me up?" Gretchen started clearing the table.

"Maybe," Michael said with a grin. "May I have dessert?"

Another glass of bourbon was slammed down in front of him. Gretchen went back to the counter and started washing the dishes. This time, since he knew he wasn't going to get another, Michael drank his requested beverage more slowly, swirling it around in his mouth and savoring the flavor. Scraping his chair back, he picked up his glass.

At the sound, Gretchen jumped, slopping some of the sudsy water onto her midriff. "Something else you need?"

"Sorry I startled you. I thought I'd try the phone. Maybe it's in order and I can call somebody to come get me."

"Who? I thought you were from Chicago?" She could've bit out her tongue. *Don't press him for details, Gretchen,* she reminded. *He told you that before dinner. No questions.*

Jeezus! I've done it again! You've got to try and keep your story straight, Hamilton. "That's right. Forgot where I was for a minute. The head's still a little foggy."

"I'll just—"

"Maybe you should—"

They started over only to interrupt each other in a repeated duet. Their shared laughter effectively lightened the tension that had built since the meal. "Ladies first," Michael invited with a sweep of his arm. "You have the floor, madam."

"I was going to suggest that you go sit down and prop up your feet." She responded to his engaging smile. Unlike the cold, threatening manner he'd taken on before they'd eaten, he'd reverted to his more charming self, making her feel comfortable again. There was no longer a closed look about him, but an open honesty, some indefinable quality about him that made her want to trust him. His blue eyes twinkled with a humor she sensed was never far from the surface, and by the laugh lines near his mouth she knew he loved to smile. What kind of criminal went around laughing all the time?

"Your turn." She conceded the floor with a flourishing sweep of her own, accompanied by a slight curtsy.

"That's what I was going to say. I'll just watch a little TV or something." He started for the living area then turned back. "That is, unless you want me to earn my keep and help you with the dishes."

"That won't be necessary. There aren't many to do. Thanks for offering, though." She plunged her hands back into the sudsy warm water to hide their shaking. Before dinner she'd been shaking out of fear, but now she was shaking because of her body's response to him. *Damn those dimples, anyway!* She dropped the casserole dish into the water and began scrubbing at it.

You've got to get consistent in your thinking about this man, she lectured at the crusted remains of sweet potato stuck stubbornly to the dish. He's either a perfectly innocent victim of his own stupidity or some sort of crook. Looking up, her eyes settled on the radio. Glancing at the clock she saw that it was almost seven. The news would be on. If there'd been an escape from the Chillicothe Correctional Institution or anyplace else, it would be announced. She flipped on the dial, keeping the volume fairly low.

Over her shoulder she could see Mack ensconced on her camelback sofa. His back was to her and he was watching television. For once the reception was fairly good. A national news program was just ending and the visit of some foreign dignitary at the White House was being covered. Gretchen doubted a story about a prison escape in central Ohio would make it to the national level, so she went back to the radio.

As the music ended, the announcer began giving a short evening report. There was nothing about a prison break or anything else that might apply to the man she'd found by the swamp. Somewhat relieved, Gretchen finished the dishes, dried her hands, and went into the living area. Mack was no longer on the couch, but had pulled back one of the curtains of the front windows and was peering, intently, out into the darkness.

At her entrance Rocky thumped his tail in friendly greeting and Mack instantly dropped the curtain, spinning around. Frowning slightly, Gretchen asked, "Looking for someone?"

"No, just curious about what's outside." Michael shoved his hands into his back pockets and sauntered back to the couch. He'd thought he'd heard tires crunching over gravel, and his heart had skipped a beat. Fortunately, there had been nothing. Rocky hadn't moved and Michael took that for a good sign. He no longer thought of the dog as much of a threat to himself, but believed the beast would alert him to anyone prowling around outside.

He fiddled with the channel selector knob on the television, then asked, "Anything special you want to watch?"

Gretchen moved toward her loom. "No, I was going

81

to weave some more. Watch anything you like. There's a copy of the Sunday issue of the *Columbus Sentinel* in the basket beside the couch. The weekly program listings should be in it."

Michael looked at the stacked up newspapers in the large basket as if they were a nest of snakes. She did get the *Sentinel!* Why hadn't she said anything about Mack Dawson? If she read the paper at all, she couldn't have missed all the hoopla that had been made about the detective series. He picked up the issue and saw a small reminder at the top of the front page informing the reader where the series could be found and that this week featured the exciting fourth chapter.

"You only get the Sunday paper down here?" he asked, keeping his voice steady as he made a show of leafing through the paper as if he weren't familiar with it.

"I could get it every day, but it would be a day late, so I just pick up a Sunday edition at the drugstore. The radio and television keep me pretty well informed." She checked the shuttle to make sure it was full. Satisfied, she positioned herself on the bench, looked over the design that was taking form, and began to weave.

Michael couldn't stand the suspense. "This looks like a pretty good paper. You read much of it?"

Gretchen pulled the beater snugly against the row of creamy yarn she'd just shot through the warp threads. "I try to keep up on the national and state news. I've never been much for reading a newspaper from front page to last. Why?" She shifted her feet on the treadle and readjusted the harness of the loom.

"Just wondered. No reason." Michael folded the first section of the newspaper so that the front page couldn't be seen and buried it in the basket.

5

For once Michael had absolutely no interest in the professional football game being played on the flickering television screen just beyond his feet. He kept glancing at the telephone hanging on the wall a few feet from Gretchen's loom. He wondered how he could continue checking to see if service had been restored without arousing more of her suspicions. He'd already gotten up several times, as if to stretch his muscles, and casually looked out the windows. Each time he could feel her eyes on him. She was watching him like a hawk. He was certain her imagination was running wild.

She wasn't alone in that. His imagination was driving him crazy. Every few seconds he thought he could hear an approaching car, footsteps, something prowling around outside. God, the unfamiliar sounds of the country were nerve-racking. He'd never complain about city noises again.

Cars, trucks, buses, sirens, they all meant people and there was some element of safety in a crowd. At least you didn't feel so isolated and vulnerable. Out here, there was nothing. He didn't even have his gun. . . .

"Gretchen. You didn't happen to see my gun when you found me, did you?"

"No. It must've fallen into the swamp. You might want to look for it tomorrow." Her tone was matter-of-fact and dismissive, making it clear she didn't want more conversation.

The Browns finally drove the last yard over the goal line, but the score didn't bring Michael's usual jubilation. Tonight, watching twenty-two men fight over an odd-shaped ball seemed utterly ridiculous. Taking in a game, cracking a few beers with the guys had always been his idea of a fun evening. But tonight, whether or not the Cleveland Browns made it to the Super Bowl was completely unimportant. He had bigger things on his mind. Matters of life and death.

Michael watched Gretchen's rhythmic movements as she continued to toss a little doodad across the loom and pull a part of the mechanism toward her. Looked pretty boring to him, but it held her interest for hours. He wondered if she'd be so complacent if he told her there might be a killer lurking outside her cabin window.

Perversely, he wanted to tell her and shake her up a little bit. Misery loved company, he supposed, and he *was* miserable. Gretchen could've taken his mind off his troubles by indulging him in a bit of pleasant conversation, but she seemed determined to shut him out, behaving as if he weren't even there. Mack Dawson would never have stood for it and Michael Hamilton wasn't going to either.

Thrusting his hands into his pockets, he walked

toward her and peered over her shoulder. "What are you making?"

"A coverlet." Gretchen didn't falter in her movements. Her feet continued to work the treadles, her hands busy with their assigned tasks.

"You must like these coverlets," he remarked satirically, calling attention to the half dozen or more that hung neatly over a wooden rack. "Are you making a lifetime supply or Christmas presents?"

"Neither," she answered absentmindedly as she concentrated on the pattern emerging between the weft threads. "Weaving is what I do for a living."

"I thought you were a nurse," Michael commented, baffled by her explanation.

Gretchen pulled the beater back with more force than necessary to pack the threads before swiveling on the bench to face him. "I am, or rather, was. I needed a change and moved out here."

"Why?" His keenly observant blue eyes were watching her intently.

This was a subject Gretchen had no intention of discussing. Unfortunately she couldn't think of an answer that would forestall his curiosity and her hesitation only increased it.

"You ran away, didn't you?" he probed. "From what? A man?"

She grew increasingly uncomfortable under his continued scrutiny, but then her discomfort switched to annoyance. "You won't give me information about yourself, so why should I?"

His gaze narrowed and a muscle twitched in his jaw as he set his mouth in a firm line. "I suppose that's only fair." He shrugged his shoulders and stepped up beside her. With one hand, he nonchalantly fingered the threads of her loom. "Since there's nothing else to do, why don't I use my imagination?"

"Fine," she bit out. "Because I'm not telling you anything."

"I'll just guess, then," he announced with a maddening grin. His blue eyes snapped at her as he continued, "Why would a pretty young woman live the life of a hermit out in the middle of nowhere? Why would she throw away a career in order to spin and weave in a cabin in the woods? Has to be a man," he concluded smugly.

"No, it's not." She couldn't prevent the denial even though she'd just told him she wasn't going to tell him a thing.

Michael preferred the spark of anger he saw in her eyes to the indifference he'd suffered most of the evening. It was infinitely better than seeing her fear. Dealing with her anger would at least take his mind off his own fears which had begun to suffocate him. "If it wasn't a man, it was something else. Something to do with nursing."

Anger brightened the gold in her eyes. "You have no right," she said through clenched teeth.

He'd hit on the truth or something very close to it, of that he was sure. "No, maybe I don't, but I'm going to pull it out of you anyway." Strangely he felt a great sense of relief that she hadn't run from some man. He didn't want to think of any man hurting his partridge, even though he was doing it himself.

That spark of life in her eyes was beginning to burn brighter and Michael fanned it. "You must have discovered you didn't have the stomach for dealing with the sick, maybe the dying," he jabbed brutally. "Instead of living with it, putting your training to good use, you ran away like a coward and decided to live in another century."

Gretchen came off her weaver's bench in a fury. "Stop it!" She curled her hands into fists, holding them rigidly at her sides. Every inch of her was bristling. "You don't know what you're talking about. You don't know what it was like. I'm not a coward, dammit!"

"No, I don't think you are." His voice was calm, but an infuriating smile still turned up the corners of his mouth. "But you still ran, didn't you?"

"Don't try to analyze me unless you're willing to come up with some answers yourself." Gretchen stated each word steadily and firmly. Her mouth closed tightly, and she turned away from him to stare into the flickering flames licking at the logs in the fireplace.

Michael had gotten the reaction he wanted. There was some satisfaction in knowing she wasn't really frightened of him anymore. She couldn't be or she wouldn't have gotten so angry and challenged him to tell her about himself. In the process of getting her to overcome her fears, he'd also made her anything but indifferent. She might have her back turned, but she was reacting to him. He'd been a loner most of his life, shying away from anything more than superficial relationships, but he didn't want Gretchen, the fluffy little partridge who'd rescued him, to ignore him.

She bent and tossed another log onto the fire. "Are you running, too, Mack?" she retaliated softly. "Were you trying to get away from something, hunting all by yourself in the middle of the Ohio hills?"

He supposed he could make up something to tell her, but he was sick of lying and he wasn't that good at it anyway. "Gretchen . . ." he began in a placating tone, reaching for her shoulders but dropping his hands to his sides when she shied away from him.

"Don't you dare touch me," she ground out bitterly.

Michael immediately regretted his grilling. "I wish I could explain myself to you right now, but I can't. Maybe sometime, soon, but not tonight. I know you've got no reason to trust me, but that's what I'm asking. Believe me, it's for your own good."

She stoked the fire with the poker, keeping her back to him. "I don't really have any choice, do I?"

"No," he said, detecting a slight thaw in her tone. "I'll stop digging for answers if you'll turn around and talk to me. I'm too used to the city, I guess. This silence is making me nervous and I lashed out at you."

"I guess I can understand that. When I moved out here it took me a while to get used to the country noises, too." She turned around and braved a look at him, surprised by his anxious expression. This big, hulking man was looking at her almost like a little boy pleading for attention. She almost laughed as another comparison came to mind. He had the drooping look Rocky had whenever she scolded him.

Smiling slightly, she relaxed her frozen stance. "All right, what do you want to talk about? Our backgrounds are off limits so what does that leave, the weather, politics?"

Michael sauntered back to the couch and sat down. Patting the space beside him, he invited, "Come over here and tell me about the spinning wheel and loom."

Ignoring his invitation, Gretchen sat down on the Lincoln rocker close to the raised hearth. "I went to a craft show not long after I moved down here. The area is famous for them. These hills seem to invite craftspeople of all types, and people flock from the cities on the weekends to purchase the handmade wares as well as to enjoy the scenery."

"I think I've—" He stopped himself just in time. He'd been about to blurt out that he'd heard about the craft shows in Hocking Valley. One of the women in the newsroom had been raving about them, showing off the handknit sweaters she'd purchased for every member of her family.

He cleared his throat and finished with, "I've heard of things like that in Illinois. Seems to be an age of interest in the folk crafts of the past."

"Must be a national interest, then. Not something we have just in Ohio." Gretchen tucked her feet beneath her. This conversation had to be boring him. He wasn't the type to sit still very long, and a discussion of centuries-old crafts was far too tame for a man who exuded so much vitality. Still, he'd asked for it, and talking about anything was better than the strained silence they'd endured for the greater part of the evening.

"People make all kinds of things around here. We have almost an artists colony, I suppose. There are painters, potters, sculptors and all kinds of wood crafters. A man not far from here makes absolutely beautiful clocks and other pieces better than anything you'd find manufactured commercially."

She propped her chin in her hand, warming to the topic. "People around here make things in the old ways and they make them to last. The pace is slow but steady and there's a great reward in creating something of heirloom quality."

Michael's reporter skills were working. What Gretchen didn't realize was how much about herself she was revealing. To get information sometimes it was far more effective to take the oblique approach. He might not be able to find out what drove her to this hermit's life, but he was going to discover what she saw in it. He relaxed against the high back of her couch and spread his arms along the wooden trim.

"Is that what you want?" he asked. "To create something lasting?"

"I don't know, maybe. It's just relaxing and I need that. I knitted at first, something I've done for years. A shop in Logan took everything I made and wanted more than I could produce."

She gave a wry grin. "Knitting stopped being relaxing. I saw a weaving demonstration at one of the shows and signed up for a course. I like it better and it's also a little faster. I've still got more orders than I'd like, but I can do it."

She looked back at the loom and a frown marred her smooth features. "That is, I can fill them if someone weren't distracting me."

"Sorry," he apologized with a low chuckle. "I didn't realize what I was interrupting. I thought you were just making more feathers to line your nest," he teased, humor urging his dimples to perform their magic.

Gretchen's own mouth trembled with amusement as she strove for an indignant ring in her voice. "I think there's been quite enough smart remarks about my bed."

Sliding her feet out from under her, she placed them on the floor and curled her palms over her knees. Fixing him with a look, she pronounced, "And you can stop comparing me to a plump little bird."

His laughter, deep, warm, and rich, floated across the space between them. "I can't help it. It's not a derogatory comparison, you know. I'm developing quite an interest in soft, golden birds.''

"Hmmph" was her only response as she stood up and went back to her loom. "All right, Dimple Cheeks, laugh if you must, but this bird has things to do."

She settled herself once again into the proper sequence of motions, checked the directions she'd tacked on the wall nearby, and set the loom into action. With her back to him, she allowed her smile to spread across her face. It really wasn't all that bad to be called a partridge, especially when it came from Mack.

After that the silence in the room was almost companionable. At least, Gretchen assumed so until Mack appeared once again by her side. The man couldn't seem to sit still for five minutes.

Glancing up, she noted the disgruntled look on his face. Evidently he required outside sources to keep him entertained. "Bored again?" she asked in a long-suffering tone.

"No, I'm tired," Michael stated, irritated by her condescension. She was showing the same attitude toward him as the pious sisters had at St. Andrew's School for Boys. They'd constantly corrected him for lack of patience, making the years he'd spent there seem like a prison sentence. In a way maybe that's what the court had intended, even if it had done no good. In the end it had taken a Marine drill sergeant to subdue his incorrigible behavior.

He didn't like thinking of those days either, and his question came out more testily than he'd intended. "Can you take your mind off that thing long enough to discuss our sleeping arrangements?"

Gretchen had thought of nothing else for hours, but her expression belied the fact. She gave him a cool look, then pointed to the couch. "You can arrange yourself right over there."

Eyeing the couch, Michael wasn't so sure he'd get any sleep, but maybe that was a good idea. He could stand guard all night. Nobody would be able to get into the cabin without passing him. That huge dog of hers was some comfort. Surely Rocky would bark or something if somebody tried to break in.

He ran an agitated hand through his tousled curls. "Can you tear yourself away from all this excitement you're generating long enough to get me a blanket and maybe a pillow?"

Gretchen flared at the annoyed look in his eyes. "Look, for someone who invited himself, you're certainly demanding." She slid off the bench and started toward the bedroom. "I'll be back in a second, *sir*."

Michael didn't care for the hostility in her tone. Her reservations about him appeared to be back in full swing. Well, there was nothing he could do about that now, but once he'd gotten this business settled, he was going to come back and convince her he was a very nice guy.

Hours later he still hadn't found a comfortable position on the short couch. His feet hung over the arm and he'd lost all circulation in his toes. His back felt as though it would have a permanent bend, and every time he shifted, the satiny comforter she'd given him slithered to the floor.

Worse, the silence was deafening. If it weren't for Rocky's snoring, he'd have gone out of his mind. When the last light had been switched off, it seemed that everything else had, too, including the heat. He was freezing to death.

The longer he thought about Gretchen sleeping peacefully in her nice warm nest, the more he wanted to join her there. This standing guard business was not for him. He should've remembered that from the service.

The colder he got, the more credence he gave to Rocky's protective powers. Why should he lay awake shivering all night when he had a monstrous dog lying beside the door?

Gretchen came awake with a jolt when her mattress sagged under a heavy weight and a cold draft hit her back. Seconds later an icy pair of arms wrapped themselves around her and she was pulled back against an unmistakably male body. "What are you doing in here?" she squeaked, fear drying her mouth.

"I'm cold," Michael whispered pathetically. "Don't be scared, I just want to get warm." He gave a contented sigh as the warm flannel of her gown began heating his shivering flesh.

Pulling her even closer, he nudged her into a fetal position. He slid his arm beneath her and fit himself against her back. Her buttocks were pushed into his cold belly and her legs were caught between his.

He might say he had nothing on his mind except getting warm, but Gretchen had evidence of something more. She could feel a probing hardness against her and tried to squirm away. She should have refused to let him stay the night, but now it was too late. If he tried to take her, there was nothing she could do.

"Please," she begged. "Leave me alone."

"I can't, little partridge. I need your warm feathers, and besides, this nest is more than big enough for the both of us."

He sounded sincere, and considering all that had

happened to him, it would seem probable that sleep in a warm bed might be all he had on his mind. Her fears lessened, slightly, at the sound of his even breathing, but she was still tense. Never thinking he'd see her in it, she'd pulled on her favorite nightshirt and nothing else.

Old and worn, the soft flannel garment only came to her knees, was slit on each side and already riding high on her thighs. If she moved a muscle, there'd be nothing between them but his briefs. It had taken her only seconds to determine that was all he had on. Her concerns were not only with the negligible length of her shirt but with the gaping front. The ribbon tie that gathered the neck together had come undone and the opening slashed deep between her breasts.

His arms were around her ribcage, but with little movement on either of their parts, her breasts would spill into his hands. Her nipples went hard with the thought. She had even more reason to be afraid. Her body was betraying her and if he became aware of it, something more than sleep could very well follow.

She swallowed hard to stifle the hysterical giggles that threatened to erupt. It was complete lunacy. Gretchen Stockwell, who generally preferred a good book to a blind date, was in bed with a man she suspected of being a criminal. What's more, her body was actually yearning for his. Her lips began to throb in memory of his kiss. A liquid warmth started from deep inside her, curling outward in ever increasing circles until she thought she would explode from the tension.

She forced herself to take deep, even breaths, match her rhythm to Mack's. Somehow she had to relax, fall asleep—anything but lie here in such torture. It would be pure madness to give in to the need that had built up inside her. By the sound of his breathing, it would appear he was asleep. He wasn't having any trouble ignoring his body's arousal, so why couldn't she?

She tried concentrating on anything else but the man who held her so snugly in his arms. Unfortunately her mind capriciously refused to produce any images except ones of Mack. His firm mouth softening into an infectious smile. Dimples forming deep grooves in strong cheeks. Mischievous lights dancing in wondrous blue eyes. Deep, hearty laughter rumbling from a wide, hairy chest. Those were the safest images projected across the back of her eyelids.

This wasn't such a good idea, Michael told himself as he tried unsuccessfully to will his body into repose. You promised her that all you wanted was a warm place to sleep, but that's never going to happen if you don't unwind your body from around hers. But yet, the last thing he wanted to do was unlock his arms and roll to the other side of the bed. Whatever it was she had on, the material seemed to work like a magnet on his hands. He couldn't move them away from the soft, brushed texture.

He'd wanted to get warm and he'd been successful. His body felt like a furnace, and the only way he could possibly cool it was to leap out of this bed and run a mile or two outside in the cold. Since he didn't have his jogging shoes with him, that didn't sound like a very good idea, nor did leaving her and taking a cold shower. The most convenient solution lay sleeping in his arms—trustingly.

Trust. That was the biggest problem. He'd asked for her trust and she'd evidently given it. It would be completely unfair to take advantage of her in her sleep. Remembering how she'd responded to his kiss, he had no doubts that she'd also respond to his lovemaking.

There'd been a spark of sexual awareness between them from the beginning. She was attracted to him, all right. Looked at him longingly all the time. Well, most of the time. Well, maybe only part of the time, he amended reluctantly. When she wasn't scared half out of her wits or completely ignoring him, he'd seen the signs. A man knew when a woman desired him, and Gretchen did . . . didn't she?

If she didn't want him in bed with her, wouldn't she have screamed for that dog? If she were really scared, she wouldn't feel so relaxed in his arms. Wouldn't be wiggling that gorgeous bottom against him like she was doing now. The partridge was a little reserved, but maybe this was her way of initiating something.

Michael lay there pondering for only a few more moments. He'd give her a chance. If she were asleep, he'd leave her alone and find the strength to get out of this bed, but if she were awake . . .

"Gretchen?" he whispered softly, nuzzling his lips in her hair just beyond her ear.

"Mmmm," Gretchen managed from between the teeth she'd clamped over her lips to stop their throbbing.

That was all the encouragement Michael needed. Not wanting to frighten the partridge from the nest, however, he cautioned himself to go slowly, gently. He flicked the tip of his tongue across her ear and Gretchen's resulting squirm rewarded him with soft full breasts spilling into his waiting hands. Her nipples shied from the contact, tightened and poked his palms.

"Oh, Gretchen," he groaned.

He slithered his lips moistly down her neck, pressing short hungry kisses along the way. Turning her slightly in his arms, he nibbled a line up her throat, along her chin, the corner of her mouth. His hands gently kneaded the wondrous fullness he held while his legs brushed against hers.

Gretchen was lost to the gentleness she sensed in this big man who held her. She didn't feel trapped but rather, sheltered. He was going to make love to her unless she extricated herself right now from the sensual cocoon he was spinning around her, but everything female in her wanted to stay.

He wasn't forcing her. He was inviting her to join him in a mating dance that required her as a partner. Gretchen accepted the invitation, instinct overriding her common sense, guiding her to respond.

She lifted her hands to the back of his, encouraging his caressing by pressing them into her breasts. Her palms registered their masculine texture. Fascinated by the contrast of hard cords of muscle beneath the light sprinkling of soft hair, she ran her palms along his forearms.

Gretchen turned in his arms, eager to further explore this male body that had enticed her from the first moment. When he'd been unconscious, her touch had been professionally aloof, but now she was eager to run her hands intimately over the hard planes and angles of his powerful body. Nothing separated her from his flesh as she lay facing him in bed. When she touched his chest, the direct contact verified what she had only guessed before. He felt wonderful.

"Oh, yes, Partridge, touch me," Michael murmured against her lips, and then covered them with his own.

His tongue was sweetly coaxing as it ran along the outline of her lips. She opened to him, not needing tantalizing persuasion but wanting the full possession she remembered. He obliged her readily, swirling through her mouth.

His hands left her breast, grasped the hem of her nightshirt, and swept the flannel garment off her body. Gretchen didn't need its protection, for his heavy warmth covered her immediately. His lips parted over hers and his tongue waited for no encouragement to dip into the honeyed interior of her mouth. He sipped her sweetness until Gretchen was no longer satisfied to give but sought his taste, thirsty for the flavor of him.

His hands smoothed down her sides, curled around her hips and slid beneath her to grasp her soft derrière. Gretchen's hands were just as busy but encountered the soft cotton that still covered a fraction of him. Her fingertips slipped easily beneath the wide elastic band, leading her palms to the smooth, hard buttocks she'd clutched hours before. His arousal was hot and strong, restless behind the thin barrier.

Excited, Gretchen arched into him, pulling him tighter against her. He thrust against her and Gretchen writhed beneath him, brushing her breasts against his chest, rubbing her thighs against the insides of his.

He moved down her body, licking the tops of her breasts, the sides, underneath, then concentrated on drawing an ever smaller circle around her nipples until he finally took one into his mouth. With his tongue curled around that dusky peak, he rolled the other between his thumb and finger. He moved farther down, pressing kisses into her abdomen, her navel, and along the line of her hips, his hands moving between her legs to prepare the way.

His briefs joined her shirt on the floor just before his fingertips searched for and found the center of her desire. Alternately soothing and tantalizing, his touch sent tiny explosions of ecstasy through her. The tingling sensation that began in Gretchen's body, rose to tremors when his finger slid inside her, and built to a quivering need.

Gretchen moaned and strained into the pleasure he was giving her. "Now . . . please . . . now," she urged, more than ready for the final act.

At once Michael filled her. Gretchen's arms and legs wrapped around him, claiming as she herself was being claimed. She opened her eyes to look up at the man who'd ignited such a fever in her. In the darkness, she could see nothing but knew he was watching her. Not moving his lower body, he kissed her eyes, her nose, then settled his mouth over hers.

Slowly at first, then faster, the rhythm led them each step of the way. Her softness joined his hardness. Her fragility cradled his power. Each the antithesis of the other, but together they were the whole, partners in a duet of joy.

"Oh, Mack!" Gretchen cried in the final measure, clinging to him as her body tensed one last time before floating in the radiance of fulfillment.

At the sound of Gretchen's cry, Michael hesitated, a brief shaft of disappointment marring his joy. Michael, my name's Michael, he wanted to shout but was too inflamed to reason beyond the instincts guiding his plunging body. Out of control he drove one final time and shuddered his release. After-tremors shook them, at first strong, then lessening in intensity until they lay limp in each other's arms.

"You're a lot of woman in one small package," Michael spoke in a ragged whisper. Knowing he was probably crushing her but reluctant to break the contact, he eased his chest from hers. Supporting most of his weight on his forearms, he kissed her lightly and repeatedly as he swiveled his hips striving for and giving a sweet reminder of their oneness.

The short-lived experience of years ago hadn't prepared Gretchen for what she felt in Mack's arms. A delicious languor filled her. Any apprehensions she might have had in giving herself so totally to a man she knew next to nothing about were faint, tucked far away in her brain.

It might not be love that she felt for this man, but it was certainly more than physical attraction. Their joining had been far more than a satisfaction of sexual need. She felt too . . . cherished? There was no other word she could use to describe her feelings.

"Enough woman for you?" she asked in a drowsy murmur.

"More than enough," he answered, then rolled them both to their sides, still retaining their unity. Legs entwined, torsos separated by only a sheen of moisture, their hearts beating in harmony against each other, they fell asleep.

6

I don't have much time, Barney, so listen up. The woman will be out here any minute."

Gretchen could hear Mack's voice coming through the open crack in the bedroom door, but he spoke in such a low voice she could barely make out the words. It was a good thing she'd forgotten to take a pair of socks into the bathroom with her this morning, or she wouldn't have known he was using the phone. It might be an invasion of privacy but this was one conversation she intended to hear. Maybe now she'd get a few answers to some very plaguing questions.

"Hell, Barney, she's no fool. I can't get away with this charade much longer" was the next thing she heard Mack say as she stealthily opened the door a bit wider. Charade?

As Mack listened to whatever Barney something or other was saying, Gretchen swallowed the gathering lump of fear in her throat. She peeked through the crack, her pulses picking up speed as she noted Mack's furtive stance and his nervous glances at the closed bathroom door. It was patently obvious that he didn't want her to walk in on his conversation.

"I need money," Mack said in a fervent whisper, cupping the receiver in his hand. There was a long pause, then, "Are you nuts? I'm in enough trouble without adding stealing to the list."

Gretchen breathed a short-lived sigh of relief that was promptly turned into a strangled gasp. Even though Mack's tone was quiet, it was deadly intense. "I'm not taking her with me unless there's no other choice. Why would she talk to the cops? Unless I follow your advice and rip off her purse and car, I can walk out of here with her none the wiser. No way. I've behaved like an angel so far and I don't want to tarnish my image."

Mack had a warped conception of angelic behavior, but Gretchen was too frightened to dwell on that very long. Moreover, losing her virtue *did* seem like nothing compared to losing her life.

"What do you want me to do?" Mack breathed angrily. "Knock her over the head?" He paused as if waiting for another directive. "Well . . . maybe. . . ."

Gretchen's heart began catapulting inside her chest. She'd heard enough. Discovering that Mack looked down on stealing was little comfort in the face of an even greater threat. She glanced down at her bathrobe, then dashed quickly into the bathroom and began pulling on her clothes. Thank God she'd left the water running in the tub. He'd think she still hadn't started her bath.

To lend credence to that belief, she shouted loudly. "Mack, would you mind turning up the dial on the water heater? I can't get enough hot water. It's in that little pantry off the kitchen.''

After a few moments Mack called back, "Be glad to. Just a second.''

Gretchen pictured him trying to decide whether or not to hang up before going to do her bidding. She didn't much care what he did so long as he believed she'd be spending a good deal more time in the bathroom. As soon as she heard his footsteps heading toward the kitchen, she crept back into the bedroom and threw a heavy knit sweater on over her shirt.

What a fool she'd been! When Mack had offered to make breakfast while she luxuriated in a bath, she'd thought he was trying to be considerate. There'd been some very uncomfortable moments when she'd woken up to find him beside her. It was one thing to have fallen in with his romantic seduction but quite another to face him first thing in the morning.

Having lived so long by herself, she was totally unprepared for that intimacy. She'd been grateful to him for soothing her nerves with an easygoing manner that had endeared him to her. Now the low-down swine was contemplating her demise. He'd gotten what he wanted from her, so now she was expendable.

She tiptoed toward the window that faced the back of the cabin. Every time a board creaked beneath her feet, her heart shrank in terror. Every foot seemed like a mile as she pictured Mack charging in and blocking her escape. By the time her fingers finally trembled along the flat sill, she felt faint.

With agonizing slowness she unlocked the window and pulled up the storm. Seconds later, she was lifting the last barrier of glass that remained between herself and freedom. Was it her imagination, or was the grating sound of the frame in the metal grooves loud enough to wake the dead?

She didn't wait around long enough to find out, but swiftly thrust one jean-clad leg through the opening. She couldn't feel the ground with her foot and ducked her head under the frame so she could judge her distance. Less than six inches to go.

Trying not to make a sound, she clung to the windowsill with one hand, then wishboned her legs. She sighed with relief when the toe of her shoe made contact with the hard ground. She'd made it!

She was pulling her remaining foot off the sill when a large hand closed over her ankle. In paralyzed horror, she watched her fingers being pried off the sill and taken in a firm grasp.

"Sorry, Partridge." Mack's head poked through the open window. "I can't let you do this."

Although he had to be aware that her position was painful, he didn't let go of her. She'd seen ballerinas stand with one foot elevated to a bar but she'd had no such training and felt like she was being split in half. Even so, she tried to pull away, but that only caused her to lose her balance. Like an ungainly pendulum, she teetered to one side. Her upper body slammed against the side of the house as her foot frantically searched for another hold.

"Ouch!" she cried out in pain, almost shouting with gratitude when he let go and swiftly thrust her foot off the sill. Unfortunately, though both feet were now planted on the ground, there was a shooting pain in her arm that, because of his hold, was twisted at an awkward angle.

"Please," she pleaded hoarsely, unable to stem a rising hysteria. "Let me go. I won't tell the cops you were here. I promise. You can have all my money, my car. Just let me go. Don't hurt me."

She didn't see the stricken look in his eyes, was aware of nothing but the unrelenting hold on her wrist. She planted her feet on the bottom log of the cabin and pulled back, hoping the additional leverage would help her break away from him.

"I don't want your money, Partridge, and I'm not going to hurt you," Mack promised in a harsh tone. "Let me help you back in here. Then we can talk. I thought it was better to keep you in the dark, but I never dreamed . . ." His voice changed and became much more tender. "You don't have to be scared of me, Gretchen. Honest."

"Then let go of my arm." Her voice wavered on a bubble of panic.

He looked pained but refused to let go, shaking his head. "You don't understand. I can't risk you running off and telling the wrong people I'm here, but that doesn't mean I'm a . . . a what? A thief? A murderer?" A glimmer of hurt shone in his eyes. "Is that what you really think?"

"I heard you on the phone," she accused, even knowing it was a stupid admission. What if he'd done something so horrible that he couldn't afford to leave behind anyone who could identify him? There was nothing appealing about his expression now. No dimples. No laughter in his blue eyes. She'd been wrong to trust him on such a foolish basis.

In desperation she clawed at his arm with her free hand, digging her nails into his wrist. She heard his muffled curse, but didn't heed the warning until her fingers were firmly grasped together and he was pulling her up off her feet.

"No!" she cried. "Damn you. No!"

Gretchen did everything in her power to keep from being dragged back through the window, but she quickly lost the battle. He was too big, too strong, and she was helpless to stop him. With one large hand grasping the waistband of her jeans, he swiftly hoisted her over the sill. She didn't stop struggling even then, and still didn't stop when he dropped her on the bed and came down on top of her.

Trying hard not to hurt her, Michael pinned Gretchen's thrashing legs beneath his thighs, and pulled her arms over her head so her clawing fingers couldn't lash out at his face. He already sported enough scratches on his arms. She might be small but she fought like a cornered animal and had almost landed several kicks in some highly sensitive areas.

He kept telling himself he was doing this because she was hysterical and giving him no choice, but it didn't alleviate his guilt. Because she'd overheard his phone call, this plucky woman believed she was fighting for her life. Manhandling her was only going to make it harder to convince her otherwise.

He pressed her down in the mattress, waiting until he felt her go limp beneath him and heard her gasping for breath. Keeping hold of her wrists, he lifted his chest so she could take in some air. "If you promise to listen to me, I'll let you up," he said in the most gentle tone he could muster.

Her eyes were huge, the pupils dilated to twice normal size. Her face had practically no color and for a moment he thought she was going to faint. He couldn't prevent a thankful grin when she finally said something, even though it was only one word and extremely foul.

"Such language," he scolded, but Gretchen knew

he'd taken no offense. She was astonished when he threw his leg to one side, sat up on the edge of the mattress, and then pulled her into a seated position beside him. He retained his hold on her wrists and she glared at her captured hands.

"I'm not giving you the chance to hurt me some more," he said pointedly, nodding toward the red streaks on his arm. "I didn't know my partridge would have such sharp talons."

"I'm not your anything," Gretchen retorted heatedly, surprising herself by her own courage. She might be in the hands of a felon, but she wouldn't be a meek and pliant victim. She had saved this man's life.

Surely he wouldn't pay her back with brutality. For some reason she actually believed him when he'd said he didn't want to hurt her. Reflecting on what had just happened, she realized he could've done far worse than hold her down. Seated beside him, thigh to thigh, her head only reaching to his shoulder, she was alarmingly aware of his massive size.

"This really hurts," he accused as he studied his wounds.

It was difficult to be frightened of a man who behaved like a young boy whining over a playground injury. He was making a blatant appeal to her sympathies, and even though she knew better than to fall for it, it had an effect. No matter what he was, the damned man was a master at bringing out her maternal instincts.

A perplexed frown developed on her forehead as she took in the deepest scratch she'd delivered to his arm. She'd actually drawn blood! "I . . . I'm sorry about that. I was so scared, I didn't know what I was doing."

"I know." Michael shrugged off her apology. "When I tell you the whole story, you probably won't be sorry." He gave her a searching look. "Will you listen to my explanation before going at me again?"

Listening to him wouldn't cost her anything, so she agreed. He let go of her hands and she quickly pulled them into her lap and began massaging her wrists to restore circulation.

"I wasn't holding on that tight, was I?" Michael asked, another surge of guilt twisting his stomach.

Gretchen saw the genuine concern on his face and it increased her confusion. Mack appeared more upset at having hurt her than she was. He made a strange kind of crook if that's what he was. His blue eyes seemed to beg for understanding and forgiveness.

Once again, a strong nurturing streak in her came to the surface and without realizing what she was revealing, she soothed, "We partridges have bird bones you know. Large beasts like yourself have to be extra gentle with us fragile creatures."

Twin dimples peeked out from the deep grooves in his cheeks. "I can be gentle. Didn't I show you that last night?"

Gretchen wasn't prepared for any reference to their lovemaking. It was something she'd much rather not think about. "Let's get back to the matter of a certain incriminating phone call, Mack Dawson. Who's this Barney person and why did he suggest you steal my money and car?"

"Not steal," Michael amended quickly. "Borrow."

His expression became repentant—or as repentant as a man can look when he has to control a set of mischievous dimples. "It was a dumb idea anyway." He shrugged his shoulders and went on in a hopeful tone, "If you were listening, you heard me say so. I'm too grateful to you to do anything like that."

"I also heard you consider knocking me over the head."

Ignoring the possible consequences of admitting how much she'd heard, Gretchen charged, "That doesn't sound much like gratitude to me."

The sight of Mack's wince gave her an odd sense of security. Even though she was the intended victim of at least two crimes, she felt less threatened with each passing second. There was something about Mack that made her want to trust him, believe in him, and it wasn't just his incomparable lovemaking.

He'd scared her more than once since they'd met, but her instincts always told her she had little to fear. It was almost as if he were two men. At times he was gentle and funny, sensitive and endearing, but at other times he was ruthless and aggressive, intimidatingly virile. She chose to believe that the gentle funny man was the real Mack Dawson and that he'd resorted to aggression because of the situation he found himself in, a situation she had yet to understand.

"I know how that must have sounded, but I wouldn't have hit you unless I was forced into it." Michael was determined to be honest, but seeing her appalled expression, he hastily tacked on, "I mean . . . that would've been a last resort if things got way out of hand."

"Am I supposed to be relieved?" Gretchen arched one brow in sarcastic inquiry. "What kind of man goes around knocking out women, and who'd force you to do something like that? Barney?" Her mind ran wild with the possibilities but her voice remained calm. "You were shot, weren't you, Mack? You didn't have an accident with your gun?"

"No, it wasn't an accident." Michael stood up from

109

the bed, then turned and looked down at her. He jammed his hands into the front pockets of his fatigues and began pacing up and down the floor.

She could tell some internal struggle was going on as she waited patiently for him to elaborate. After a few minutes it looked as if he'd forgotten all about her, so she urged softly, "Mack. Tell me what this is all about."

He stared at her for a few seconds, then seemed to make up his mind about something. "To begin with. My name's Michael Hamilton, not Mack Dawson. I made him up."

"You made him up," she repeated, trying not to show how much the information shocked her. He'd done nothing but lie to her since the first moment they'd met. What else was a lie? The feeling she'd imagined in him last night? Was that a lie, too?

"Go on," she encouraged, fighting down the sick feeling in the pit of her stomach.

She must not have disguised her reaction as well as she'd hoped because he commanded gruffly, "Don't look at me like that, Gretchen. I only did it to protect you. If anyone asked you about Michael Hamilton, you would've said you didn't know anyone by that name. Of course, anyone who reads the *Sentinel* would recognize Mack Dawson, so it was a stupid name to pick, but my brain wasn't working very well at the time."

"The *Columbus Sentinel*?" she asked, and tried to think if she'd read anything lately that should have tipped her off to his subterfuge before now. She'd thought the name had sounded familiar. With a sudden jolt of memory, she recalled where she'd heard it before.

"Mack Dawson! That hard-nosed comic-strip hero in the detective serial, right?"

At almost the same time she remembered some of Mack's—or Michael's—more obnoxious behavior. His seemingly split personality had an amazingly simple explanation. "And you didn't just adopt the name, did you? All that macho stuff yesterday was an act, too, wasn't it? Just to scare me?"

She couldn't help herself. She started to laugh, and the offended look on Michael Hamilton's face just made her laugh harder.

"It's not that funny," he bit out. "I did scare you, so I must have been convincing in the role."

He had a very good point, and it suddenly dawned on her that his posing as a fictional private eye had little to do with the seriousness of the situation. The man had been shot and he was afraid of the police. Mack or Michael. He was in some kind of serious trouble, and because she'd found him, it was highly possible that she was, too.

Her last giggle died an abrupt death. "And I'm still scared, Ma . . . Mr. Hamilton." She frowned. "That's not another alias, is it?"

Exasperation tightened every muscle in his big body. "No, it's not and the name is Michael. Don't you dare call me Mr. Hamilton. We've slept together, for Chrissake."

"I slept with Mack Dawson," she reminded him testily. "According to the paper, that only makes me one of thousands of other women. For that reason I'm not putting any special meaning on it. He wouldn't."

"Damn you, Gretchen!" he shouted. "You're deliberately trying to—"

A startled look came over his face and he stalked swiftly away to the open window. He gazed outside, then quickly darted back out of sight, flattening himself against the wall. "You know anyone who drives a blue Chevy?" he hissed.

"No." She got off the bed, intending to look out the window herself, but Michael pulled her away before she could see anything or be seen. He held her by the shoulders in front of him, and unlike the last time she'd been in his grasp, she wasn't the least bit frightened. "It's probably one of my neighbors, Michael. Calm down."

Even though she'd assumed his personification of Mack Dawson was purely for effect, she now learned otherwise. Michael's eyes were cold, his expression grim. "Take a quick look and tell me what you see. Don't let them see you."

It was a command, pure and simple, and Gretchen instantly obeyed. "It looks like the sheriff," she stated quietly.

Against her back she could feel him tense, then relax. "God, now what do I do?" she heard him whisper, but sensed he was asking himself, not her. "Don't move." Now, that was for her. Again she obeyed and remained still as he leaned toward the window, lifted the curtain, then immediately let it drop back into place.

The local sheriff hadn't come alone, but had brought two passengers. Grimes and Mosher. Michael knew he was trapped with only one thing standing between himself and another life. Gretchen.

Gretchen gave a startled gasp when he grabbed her elbow and began pulling her across the room. At the bedroom door he turned her around and pushed her shoulders against the wood. He looked down into her eyes and she'd never seen such desperation on any-one's face.

"I'm begging you, Partridge. Don't tell them I'm here. Unless you want my blood on your hands, go out there and act natural."

"But Sheriff Townsend's a nice man," she breathed, trying to convince him to do the only right thing. If he'd done something wrong, he should turn himself in. "He'd try to help you, Michael. I know he would."

"No."

The softly spoken word was painfully final. She lifted her chin to read the expression in his eyes, her lower lip quivering with what she saw. He was giving her a burden far too heavy to handle. "Michael, I can't—"

The loud knock on the front door brought Rocky awake with a barrage of barking. Michael pulled Gretchen to him and gave her a brief kiss on the lips, a kiss so sweet it pulled on every feminine nerve.

"Trust me, Partridge," he whispered, then stepped away and pushed her through the door. It closed behind her with a quiet click.

Gretchen's legs were shaking as she stumbled toward the front door. Her heart was thudding like a kettle-drum and her body was covered by gooseflesh. If she opened the door in this state, the man outside would immediately know that something was wrong.

"Down, Rocky!" she ordered her dog, who was standing up on his two hind legs, his front paws on the door. As the dog dropped back to all fours, she drew in a deep breath, then lifted the latch.

"Sit, Rocky," she said over her shoulder before facing the heavyset man who stood on her doorstep. "Good morning, Sheriff. Can I do something for you?"

Although her face felt like it was cracking, she offered

a smile to the two uniformed policemen who stood behind the sheriff. This *was* about Michael. She could feel it, and she swallowed the large constriction in her throat.

"Maybe so, Miss Stockwell," Townsend said, his eyes straying over her shoulder and into the house. "We're looking for someone. Have you seen a strange man wandering around here yesterday or today?"

Michael leaned his head back on the bedroom door. His forehead broke out in a sweat as the spine-tingling anxiety inched up his back. He searched the room for some kind of weapon but there was nothing. His only protection was in the form of a woman, a woman who had every reason to think that she'd just been saved from a frightening ordeal.

Please, Partridge, he prayed silently. Remember what we shared last night. Let my loving make up for the words I never gave you.

"I did see someone, yes," Gretchen replied, lifting both brows. "I was a few miles out in the woods." She pointed to the trees. "I saw this man walking along the county road and he looked like he was sick or something. I called out to him."

She looked at the two other policemen. "I'm a nurse, you see, and I thought maybe I could help him."

"Pardon me, Miss Stockwell." Townsend stepped aside and gestured to his companions. "These are two of Columbus's finest. They're down here looking for a man who . . . who's wanted for—"

"Never mind, Sheriff," the larger of the two uniformed men interrupted. Both men pulled out their identification and flashed her a badge. "Can you tell us more about this man, ma'am?"

"Not much, I'm afraid," she apologized. "I was still

about twenty yards away from him when a car came down the road. It stopped for him and he got in. I just assumed he was a deer hunter who was waiting for his ride."

"Why did you think he was a hunter?" the bull-necked policeman asked.

"He was dressed like one. You know, those camouflage suits." She appeared to consider for a few seconds. "Come to think of it . . . he wasn't carrying a gun. Was he the man you're looking for?"

"Big man? Dark curly hair? Blue eyes? About mid-thirties?" The younger, wiry policeman queried as he joined the other two men on her front stoop.

Gretchen nodded. "I didn't get close enough to see his eyes though. What did he do?"

Ignoring her question, Townsend requested a description of the car the man had gone off in. She described a late model Ford she'd seen in a recent ad. "Was this man dangerous?"

"No," the older policeman shook his head, nodding the others back toward the car. "He's just another deadbeat who's trying to wiggle out on his child support payments. His ex found out he was coming here to go hunting, and we contacted your sheriff, hoping he could pick him up. Looks like the lady's out of luck."

"That's too bad," Gretchen mouthed sympathetically, though her mind was racing.

That couldn't be true, could it? No. Running out on child support payments did nothing to explain Michael's accident. She doubted very much that his supposed ex-wife had tracked him into the fields and shot him. Which meant that the police were lying. Why?

She said good-bye, then closed the door. Moments later the car backed out of her drive and she verified its leaving by watching out the front window until it had disappeared down the narrow, winding road. She didn't even jump when she heard Michael's voice behind her.

"Bless you, Partridge. If I were a movie producer, I'd make you a star."

"According to them, you're a deadbeat who's skipped out on his support payments," she said, still peering out the window. She twisted her head to look at him. "Do you have a vengeful ex-wife out there somewhere, Michael?"

"Hardly, and I'm not a deadbeat, either. I'm a nice bachelor type who holds down a steady job and pays all his bills. The only woman I send any money to is my widowed mother in Albany."

His amused grin was the final proof she needed to dismiss the policemen's farfetched explanation of Michael's crime, but now she was more determined than ever to get the real facts. By her own choice she'd just made herself an accomplice. To what, she didn't know. There was no longer any doubt that she was harboring a fugitive. Those men at her door had been very real policemen and they were definitely searching for Michael. She'd deliberately misled them!

Michael wanted to curse out loud at the stricken expression on her face. By the slight trembling in her body, he judged that she was half in shock. She'd had an awful lot to handle for one day. How could he tell her the rest? How could he stand to watch more fear come into her lovely hazel eyes?

Wanting only to offer his protection and not thinking how she might react, he turned her to face him. She didn't say a word when he gathered her into his arms.

His hand closed over the frantic pulse in her throat as he lowered his lips.

Gretchen closed her eyes. Part of her wanted to remain within the security of Michael's strong arms, savor the addicting taste of him, but another part was angry with what he'd just made her do. He'd forced her to break the law. Forced her by being the most gentle, considerate lover she could imagine.

He'd seduced her with tender words and caressing hands and played upon every one of her emotional weaknesses. He'd taken unfair advantage of the maternal, caring part of her that had prompted her to become a nurse. His soulful blue eyes and charming dimples had conspired against her until she'd foolishly thrown away all of her principles.

Michael didn't realize the woman in his arms wasn't seeking comfort until he felt her fingers pulling on the short curls at the back of his neck. He didn't realize she was angry until she'd cemented her grip and inflicted real pain.

"Hey!" he protested. She was trying to pull his hair out by the roots.

He managed to pull his lips away from hers for a second, but she'd only started what she felt was a worthy punishment. A man like him didn't deserve all those silky curls anyway, she thought nastily.

She pulled his head down and covered his open mouth with her lips. If nothing else, last night's lovemaking had taught her a few things he liked and she combined the painful jerks on his hair with the lush press of her full breasts. The tiny nips she took of his sensitive lower lip were coupled with the darting pleasure of a provocative searching tongue.

She felt a heady triumph at his confusion. He didn't know whether to push her away or beg for more. She liked him confused. It gave them something in common.

Her triumph didn't last long. In a way that would have done Mack Dawson proud, Michael reached up and took hold of her fingers. He forced her hands away from his hair and down to her sides. Pulling on her wrists, he brought her up against his surging arousal. He kept her in place with one hand firmly planted across her buttocks and used the other to unbutton the top button of her blouse.

Michael was in control of their kiss now, using his tongue and teeth to vanquish her indignant rebellion. When he lifted his mouth away, she was almost sputtering. Sparkling blue eyes glittered down at her outraged face as he undid two more buttons on her blouse, revealing the swell of her breasts.

"If you want to play it rough, I'd be happy to oblige," he informed her huskily. "I just didn't expect you to embrace the part of my moll so quickly."

"Of all the . . ." She arched her back, but that gave him easy access to the full curves he'd just exposed.

She suffered through his retaliatory seduction as best she could, trying not to gasp when he nibbled at her throat or moan when his tongue traced along the laced edge of her bra. With her eyes squeezed tightly shut, she wasn't aware he'd stopped tormenting her until she felt his fingers refastening her buttons.

"We don't have anymore time for this, Partridge." He tapped her nose with one finger. "We're blowin' this joint and goin' on the lam."

7

On the lam!" Gretchen's face mirrored her disbelief. Her hazel eyes stared up at Michael. "Are you crazy?"

Michael grabbed her by the shoulders and started propelling her toward the bedroom. "Come on, Partridge. Get a move on. I don't know how much time we've got."

Gretchen tried planting her feet firmly, but Michael just pushed her stiff body along in front of him while delivering a stacatto stream of instructions. "They could be back any minute. Throw whatever you need in a bag and let's get out of here. Bring all the money you've got on you. Give me your car keys. I'll go warm up the car."

As they reached the doorway, Gretchen made a last desperate move and braced her hands on the frame. Her stubborn resistance finally got through to Michael and he released her. Peering over her shoulder, he took in her set features with a thoroughly puzzled frown.

"What's the matter with you, Gretchen? Didn't you hear anything I said? Every second could count."

"You *are* crazy!" she cried, turning toward him but still clinging to the doorway for dear life. "I'm going absolutely nowhere with you, Michael Hamilton. How do I know you're not an escapee from the state mental institution?"

Michael's jaw tightened as he glared at her. "You don't, you'll just have to take my word for it." He reached for her elbow. "Don't just stand there, woman. Start packing!"

"Your word? Your word? I'm supposed to take your word?" She jerked her elbow out of his grasp and stomped back into the living room. "I'd have to be as crazy as you are to take your word for anything. You've done nothing but lie to me since I dragged you in here."

She whirled around and punched an accusing finger into his chest. "I've never broken a single law in my life, and suddenly, because of you, I'm aiding and abetting a fugitive. You better come up with some good explanations, Dimple Cheeks, or I'm calling the sheriff on you. I may not have believed that policeman's story about child support, but they want you for something. Now, what is it!"

Michael made another attempt to put off explanations until another time. "I'll explain later. Let's—"

"You'll explain *now!*" she shouted, pointing to a ladderback chair. "Sit down, you big lug. I'm tired of getting a crick in my neck."

Her expression was thunderous and Michael knew he'd pushed her too far. Meekly he backed down from his autocratic stance and gingerly settled himself on the caned seat. As soon as he felt the tremor in the chair's legs, he wished she'd ordered him to sit someplace else.

The couch. The rocker. Someplace other than this rickety chair. Sure that the spindly legs were about to splinter under his weight, Michael prepared to leap up at the first sound of the chair's demise.

"Now, you listen to me." Gretchen stood over him, wagging her finger not far from the tip of his nose.

"Yes ma'am," he answered, suppressing a grin. From vast experience he'd learned it was better not to laugh in the face of such genuine outrage. Leaning his head back to avoid the outstretched digit Gretchen was brandishing like a foil, he admitted, "We probably have a few minutes. I'll try to fill you in."

"You'd better," Gretchen warned, and to Michael's relief she crossed her arms. Watching her fingertip had begun to make him dizzy.

"For starters," she began, "I want to see some identification. Where do you live and what do you do for a living?"

"You know I lost my wallet, Partridge, but if you let me up I bet I can show you something that'll back up my story."

"What could you possibly show me that I haven't already seen?" Stepping completely out of character, she perused his body from head to foot. "Got your name tattooed on you somewhere, Michael?"

Michael's brows rose but he decided to ignore the sarcasm. He pointed to the basket holding the newspaper. "I'm Michael B. Hamilton. I live in Apartment 301, 6232 North Fourth, Columbus, Ohio. I'm a reporter for the *Columbus Sentinel* and I also write the Mack Dawson series. Bring the paper over here and I'll show you my by-line."

He gave her a sheepish grin. "There's even a picture of me next to my column. Surprised you didn't recognize me. I'm a local celebrity, you know. Haven't you heard of 'The City Talks'? I've been writing that thing for five years. Most people I meet are familiar with my straight-shooting candor."

"Most people you meet must not know much about you," she suggested pointedly. "Candor is not one of your more obvious assets."

Training her finger on him as if it were a gun, Gretchen backed across the room and reached for a newspaper. She'd read the "City Talks" column but wanted to verify the picture. She turned to the right page and immediately recognized the mop of dark curls over the wide brow, even if there was little other resemblance to the man presently seated in her living room.

"Hmmph," she grunted.

"So you believe me?"

"The picture's not very clear, but I guess you could be him." Suspicion was still in her eyes. "If you are, why did someone shoot you?"

"I knew too much and they wanted to blow me away."

"Oh, give me a break, Michael." Gretchen threw up her hands in disgust. "That sounds like something right out of the Mack Dawson series."

"I know it does. That's what's so incredible about the whole thing. It's like I—"

"You what? Dreamed it all up?"

Michael crossed his ankle over his knee and tried to get comfortable, but the chair began to teeter and he quickly placed his foot back on the floor. "Uh, Gretchen? Could I please sit somewhere else? I don't think this—"

Gretchen swiftly returned to his side and placed a

restraining hand on his shoulder as he started to rise. "You'll stay right where you are, buster, until I'm through with you."

Michael began to think Gretchen might've taken lessons from his old drill sergeant. Her jaw was set firmly and her orders were as rapid as machine-gun fire. He owed her an explanation, but this was not the way he'd wanted to go about it. He had planned to retain the upper hand, but this little bird had her feathers ruffled and wasn't backing down.

She really had him on the hot seat. Maybe she wasn't exactly the drill sergeant type after all. No, she was more like the Mother Superior at St. Andrew's. He'd spent a lot of time squirming in a straight-backed chair in Mother Filomena's office. The woman standing over him wasn't wearing a habit, but she had the same fire in her eyes as that God-fearing woman. At the moment she also looked quite capable of doing physical harm to his person. He wondered if she was hiding a ruler up her sleeve, ready to crack him across the knuckles.

Michael's fingers went numb as he remembered. After imparting her punishment, Mother would rail at him for a while, then take a deep breath, look heavenward, and gentle her tone. Finally she would place her hand on his shoulder and say, "Michael, why don't you use the fine brain God gave you? I know you're really a good boy. If you would only slow down a little and think before you act, you wouldn't be in trouble all the time."

Every hot-seat session had ended that way and Michael had learned just how to bring a smile to the elderly nun's face. He would promise to try harder, then smile up at her, having learned during his first week at St. Andrew's that even Mother Filomena was a sucker for his curly hair, blue eyes, and deep dimples. His promises weren't empty when he made them. He'd honestly try for a day or two, but then . . . well, he'd just burst.

"Michael! Answer me." Gretchen poked his chest again.

"Oh, sorry Gretchen. What did you ask me?"

Slowly and deliberately Gretchen repeated her question. "What could you know that would make someone want to kill you?"

"Actually, I don't really know that much. They just think I do." The chair began slowly listing to one side, and Michael sprang out of it before the loose leg completely gave way.

"Sorry, Gretchen," he apologized as his hands went to her waist and he lifted her to one side. "My body's taken enough abuse in the last twenty-four hours. I'm not adding a bruised tailbone to the list."

He curled his arm around her and guided her toward the couch. In his most soothing tone, he began, "Let's both sit down and I'll tell you all I know."

By the end of his explanation, Gretchen was openmouthed and wide-eyed. Horror curled in her stomach. She had been right not to turn him in. For once it had been better to break all the rules and follow her heart. Michael might be "hell on wheels," but he was the victim, not the perpetrator. "Those men with Townsend were the ones who shot you? The police?"

"Kind of undermines your trust in civil servants, doesn't it?" Michael fingered the bandage at his temple. "I don't think I've ever been more scared in my life. It seems that money can buy anything."

Gretchen struggled to assimilate all she'd just been told. "I've enjoyed reading the Mack Dawson series, but I had no idea it was so close to the truth. Tons? They really drop *tons* of marijuana into fields at night? Right around here?"

Michael nodded soberly. "They do. Since I now know that at least some of the city police are in on it, I couldn't take the chance that the locals might be involved. It looks like your sheriff is suspect. That's why I wouldn't let you take me to the hospital."

Gretchen gripped her hands. "Who's the leader of this whole thing?"

"That's the irony of it. I really don't know, but I had Mack Dawson going after the owner of a tennis club. I made it up, honest. Barney says—"

"Who's this Barney?"

"Barney Shultz. He's an F.B.I. agent."

Gretchen's nervousness intensified. She jumped up from the couch and started to pace. "Oh, Michael," she wailed softly, shaking her head from side to side. "This is really big, isn't it? My God!" She stopped and turned toward him, all color draining from her face.

"What's the matter?" Michael came up off the couch, alarmed by her ashen expression.

"Can you really trust this Barney? Maybe he's one of them, too. Otherwise, why would an F.B.I. agent want you to rob me, knock me unconscious, and—"

Michael pulled her into his arms, running his hand up and down her back, wanting to reassure her. "That isn't really what he suggested, and yes, we can trust him. Both of us thought it would be better if I left without telling you anything. We thought if we made it look as if I'd robbed you, Grimes, Mosher, and whoever else is out there looking for me would believe you weren't involved."

He kissed the top of her head, then set her away from him. Resting his hands on her hips, he bent down and looked directly into her eyes. "Believe me, I would never have hurt you. I only want to protect you."

Gretchen looked up at him, reading the concern in his eyes. He was asking for more from her than belief in his story. Knowing him only two days, she was supposed to trust him with her life. Inexplicably she was ready to do just that, though fear shriveled her stomach.

"Oh, Michael, I'm scared," she whispered.

"I am, too, sweetheart." He wrapped his arms around her and laid his cheek on her head. "I am, too."

They stood motionless, each imparting silent comfort to the other. Without words they bound themselves together. It was the two of them against the world, a world that seemed to have gone crazy. Even though Gretchen was terrified, she felt secure in Michael's arms. He would take care of her. She had instinctively known that all along.

Michael's voice sounded in her ear, his tone gruff. "I feel terrible about all this. I knew you deserved an explanation, but in telling you I've made you a target. I'm sorry, but I can't afford to leave you behind now, Gretchen. I'd go crazy wondering if they'd come back and hurt you. Barney wants me to lie low until he's got a handle on the situation, and that means we've got to make tracks. We can't stay here and risk their showing up again."

"If we go someplace else, will we be safe?" she mumbled weakly. "Are we only in danger if we stay here?"

"As long as they don't find out where we've gone, we'll be fine. I'm meeting Barney tonight, and he'll tell us where to go from there."

His answer came much too quickly, and Gretchen suspected he wasn't telling her everything. She had to trust that he would do what was best for both of them, but she felt a shudder run down her spine. She had to get a grip on herself. The last thing he needed to deal with was a hysterical woman.

She stiffened her spine along with her resolve. "All right," she declared in a take-charge tone. "Then, let's start being logical about this."

She lifted her chin and scolded, "You have this tendency to act first and think later, Michael, but I follow standard procedures. Now, the first thing we do is find a hotel that'll take pets."

Michael blinked. He couldn't have heard her correctly. "Pets?"

"We'll have to take Rocky with us," she explained patiently as she stepped away from him and went for a phone book.

"What are you doing?" he asked, nonplussed.

"I'm going to make reservations. You can't just drive up to a hotel and assume they'll have a room. What's called for here is a little advance planning." She opened the phone book and began riffling through the yellow pages.

Michael was hard put to know whether he should burst out laughing or start swearing. The lady was incredibly naive. But why shouldn't she be? he asked himself. I'm supposed to be the seasoned crime fighter of this twosome, at least that's how it looks on paper.

"You might as well take out a billboard, Partridge," he enlightened. "They may be monitoring the phone, and they'll be at the hotel before we are."

Gretchen dropped the phone as if it were a snake. "Oh! I never thought of that."

"That's what happens when you act first and think later." Michael gave a superior smile. "We're not going on a vacation, so the same rules don't apply. Now, this is the way I see it.

"First off, we get rid of the dog. If we're trying not to call attention to ourselves, we don't advertise. We won't be incognito if we travel with a monstrous Great Dane."

As if the beast in question understood he was the subject of their conversation, Rocky padded over to Michael and leaned heavily against his legs. Michael could almost have sworn the animal was begging not to be left behind. The pleading look in his liquid brown eyes was hard to withstand.

"For heaven's sake," Michael swore. "We can't take the dog. That's final."

An hour later Michael, Gretchen, and a drooling Rocky were packed tightly into Gretchen's compact convertible. "Of all cars, why do you own a red Fiat?" Michael groaned as he pushed a huge paw aside in order to shift into a higher gear. "We should have taken out an ad."

He cast a baleful eye at Rocky, who was semidraped over his shoulder. Sarcastically he recited an imaginary news bulletin. "Michael Hamilton and party are proceeding north on route 33. Anyone spotting a sporty red Fiat can contact their local authorities."

"I bought it for myself on my birthday," Gretchen retorted, stung by his tone. "I like it. How was I supposed to know it was going to be used for a getaway car?"

Michael lapsed into a disgusted silence as the car sped toward Columbus. Gretchen folded her arms over her chest and they sat in stony silence. He'd been behaving like a surly bear ever since he'd lost the argument over Rocky. She couldn't help it that Rocky refused to eat when left alone, and she didn't understand how Michael could be so unsympathetic. After all, according to him, they were in no real danger. What harm could it cause to bring Rocky? All he'd do was curl up on a floor somewhere and go to sleep.

If Michael hadn't been in such a bad mood, Gretchen would have tried to be more companionable. Having come to terms with her fears, she felt a twinge of excitement. She'd never done anything remotely like this in her life.

Her background inspired order, and spur-of-the-moment adventures had never had a place in her schedule. Until she'd met Michael she hadn't known there'd been an impetuous bone in her body. Quitting her job and moving to Hocking County had been the most adventurous thing she'd ever done, but even that had involved careful planning.

She was no Bonnie Parker who was lured from a dull life by the promise of excitement. And Michael? He was exciting, but he wasn't a cold-blooded killer and he made a lousy Clyde Barrows. She giggled. She was more like Meg in *Little Women* and he bore a striking resemblance to Tom Sawyer.

She was the type who made lists, was always organized, prepared for anything, and had the Girl Scout badges to prove it. Nothing, however, could have prepared her for this, and she was amazed by her own reactions. Here she was, about to check into a hotel with a relative stranger, a man who was the subject of a statewide manhunt, and instead of fearing for her life, she was actually enjoying herself. The sense of danger, the romantic overtones of the situation were oddly exhilarating. Maybe deep down, there *was* a little Bonnie Parker in her.

She glanced over at Michael and surmised that he

was still simmering over the amount of luggage she'd insisted on bringing along. Travel light, he had ordered, and in her eyes that was exactly what she was doing. He might feel comfortable spending an indefinite length of time in the same set of clothes, without requiring even so much as a toothbrush, but women needed a bit more than that.

"Are you going to pout all the way to Columbus?" she finally asked when miles had passed and there was still no sign of softening in Michael's expression.

"I'm not pouting," he grated stonily. "I'm thinking."

"Couldn't hurt." As soon as she'd said it, Gretchen felt sorry. After all, the man had been through a harrowing two days and she doubted she'd be in half as good a shape as he was if it had happened to her. She reached across the seat and patted his knee. "That wasn't very nice of me. Sorry."

"Neither one of us is in the best of moods," he agreed equitably. "Let's make a deal. For the remainder of our incarceration together, we'll agree to be civil. No low blows and if it looks like one of us is about to K.O. the other, we'll retreat to neutral corners."

"Boxing, football, hunting, crime." She counted off his interests on her fingers, casting him a teasing grin. "You have an amazing repertoire of various vernacular. I hope you plan to translate every once in a while. You may be a man's man, but you're dealing with a woman now and it looks like we're stuck with each other. If we're going to be partners, I'd appreciate it if you'd use simple English. Half the time, I don't know what you're talking about."

Michael discarded the major portion of her speech and honed in on the few words that sparked his irritation. "Who says I'm a man's man? Before you came along I hadn't had any complaints from women. I'll have you know that most women like me and you made a good show of it last night."

If not for the melting look he gave her, she would have made a face at him. He was incorrigible but he was also a feast to the eye and a tender, considerate lover. "Oh, I'll admit you have a few things going for you, but they don't require any talking," she returned meaningfully.

"Why, you brazen hussy!" He glowered down at the small hand creeping upward on the inside of his thigh. "What's come over you, Partridge?"

"I'm just trying to get into the role you've assigned me. Aren't molls kind of brassy?" She trailed her fingers along the stitched inseam of his fatigues. "How do you think I'd look in false eyelashes and maybe a platinum wig?" she inquired innocently.

"How do you think you'd look without anything?" Michael shot back, squirming beneath her touch. "Because that's what will happen if you keep this up."

"You shouldn't threaten members of your own gang, Michael. We felons can turn on you at any time. I haven't squealed yet, but they could break me."

"I thought you didn't understand the vernacular," he accused. "One of us is going a little crazy, all right, and it's not me or Rocky. What do you think, pal?" He patted the velvety muzzle resting on his shoulder. "Can we trust this broad?"

Rocky emitted a sympathetic whine. "Traitor," Gretchen snarled mockingly. "Crossed over to the other side, have you?" She glared at her pet. "The old adage must be wrong—there's no honor among thieves. I'll remember that in my memoirs."

Michael was becoming concerned. Although he appreciated Gretchen's lighthearted banter and was thrilled that she wasn't suffering any second thoughts about sleeping with him, he worried about her state of mind. This was not a fantasy they were playing out but a real-life drama. He didn't know if he should sober her up with a few facts or go along with her playacting.

He was more than halfway in love with her already, adored her for being such a good sport, but he couldn't let her get carried away. There was too much at stake here. Unfortunately, the feel of her fingers was rapidly destroying his ability to think rationally, and if she didn't stop soon, he was going to pull over and give her what she was asking for. That would be one memory he was certain she wouldn't care to put in her memoirs if she ever came back down to earth.

Nudging aside Michael's furry bodyguard, Gretchen placed her head on his shoulder. "Where's this hideout you're taking me to?"

Oh, hell, Michael thought, I might as well play along with her. "You don't need to know, sweetheart," he drawled out of the side of his mouth in a poor imitation of Humphrey Bogart. "Save that for later." He removed her hand from his thigh. "We don't know who's on our tail, so you'd better snatch a few z's while you can."

"I just love it when you talk gangster," she purred throatily. "I just know little ol' me will be safe with a big strong man like you around." Her tone might have been jesting, but she meant every word. She felt safe resting her head on his broad shoulder. He was built for comfort, and with a sigh she snuggled into the crook of his warm neck. "I'm only closin' my eyes because I trust you to keep me out of the slammer, big daddy."

He'd pushed her over the edge, he was sure. He'd

forced his partridge out of the nest and it had been too much for her. Glancing at the space behind the seat, he reappraised his thinking.

She wasn't out of her nest. She'd brought the whole damned thing with her. If he hadn't stopped her, she might even have brought that huge loom. Evidently she was prepared for a long siege. She'd brought enough clothes for an army, a twenty-pound sack of dog food, and enough yarn to knit socks for the entire population of Columbus.

At first, thinking about having her with him in a private motel room had seemed the culmination of a marvelous fantasy. He'd imagined spending the whole time in bed with her, but she'd come prepared to play Scrabble. That had put a damper on his enthusiasm, but during this drive, she'd indicated her interest in other games.

Oddly enough, he didn't think he approved, uncertain if she wanted his company or Mack Dawson's. Moreover, she'd raised questions in his mind about her own identity. Was she his comforting little partridge or the flippant femme fatale, hungry for danger?

He only had a few days to find out, because he knew that the F.B.I. would wrap matters up quickly now that they had him as a witness. The exclusive story he was going to get out of this was going to make his name in the business. As soon as the drug ring was rounded up, he was going to have his hands full keeping up with the story and wouldn't have much time for her.

With all of his heart, he hoped Gretchen wasn't too enamored of his Mack Dawson image, for he was nothing like the man. Forty-eight hours of it had already put him under tremendous strain, and her counting on him to keep it up didn't help. If only there'd been some other way. If only they'd met under other circumstances.

Gretchen feigned sleep. The day's events had taken a lot out of her, but her mind wouldn't shut off. Keeping up a brave front was nerve-racking. She wondered what Michael would do if she burst out crying and begged to go home to her mother.

Mother! She could imagine what her mother would say if she ever found out about this, but oddly enough Gretchen didn't care. She'd been what her parents wanted long enough, but now she was her own woman. Michael had been the catalyst she'd needed to break out of her complacency. She felt alive.

He'd accused her of running away, being a coward, and he'd been right, but she wasn't running anymore. All the emotions she'd contained for a lifetime and couldn't seem to express had suddenly come to the surface. Because of Michael she was feeling again, and even though that frightened her, it was also a vast relief. She *was* human, very human. She had done more laughing, crying, and loving in the past two days than in the whole six years she'd been a nurse.

Loving? She covered her tremble with a shift of her position, readjusting her head on his shoulder. Maybe love was what had prompted her to act so out of character. She was in love with Michael Hamilton, a card-carrying lunatic with the body of a professional football player, a man she'd known for only two days. Meek and mild little Gretchen had fallen for a choir-boy face and a pair of devilish dimples.

Michael was so full of life, he didn't deserve a wishy-washy woman. She didn't know if she could go on acting like a flashy gangster's moll, but she'd give it all she had. No matter how short their time together might be, she was determined to make it memorable. Someday she'd have to resume normal life, but she was a changed woman, no longer the shy partridge. Michael had given her back the means to venture out of her safe nest.

She didn't know how much time she'd have with Michael, whether he'd want her when this was all over, but if not, she'd have some lovely memories. Every moment she spent with him seemed precious. She hoped to gather enough of them to last her a lifetime, because after Michael, any other man would be dull.

8

⚬⚬⚬⚬⚬⚬⚬⚬⚬⚬

A garish neon sign blinked red, yellow, red, and yellow, advertising hourly rates. "You can't be serious." Gretchen stared through the windshield at the tawdry L-shaped building and the astonishingly full parking lot adjacent to it. "Tell me this is just the place where we're going to meet Barney."

"Nope." Michael wheeled the car into the parking lot and neatly jockeyed into the tight space between two sedans. "This little car does have its advantages," he announced happily as he switched off the ignition. "Busy place, isn't it?"

"God knows why." Gretchen slunk down farther in the seat. It didn't matter that there was no one around who could recognize her; she was dying of embarrassment. "There's not an empty space in the lot."

"It's probably lunch hour," Michael stated smoothly as if that explained everything.

After a momentary pause, Gretchen covered her face with her hands and groaned, "Ugh!"

Michael chuckled and pulled down on the door handle. "Wait here, I'll go check us in."

"You'll do no such thing," she whispered frantically, her eyes darting from side to side to make certain no one had noticed their arrival. "Don't you dare get out of the car and leave me alone out here. Don't you realize what sort of clientele this kind of place attracts?"

"Sure." He shrugged. "People just like us who want to keep a low profile. Cheer up, Partridge. This could be fun. Ever slept in a waterbed underneath a full . . . ah . . . harvest mirror?"

"Mirrors?" She shot him a horrified look. "That's disgusting!"

"Have you lost your sense of adventure?" Michael quirked his brow. "They've even got X-rated movies for our viewing pleasure." He pointed to the billboard that sported several other dubious distinctions offered by the management. The Twin Hills Motel provided much more than rooms. "It won't be dull. I can promise you that."

"I'm not budging an inch from this car," Gretchen warned. "Not until you explain why we have to stay in a dump like this."

"I thought that would be obvious," Michael remarked calmly. "No one here will ask any questions or wonder about our canine companion. I don't have any first-hand knowledge of this kind of institution, you understand, but I've heard that even stranger guests have been known to check in. I heard about this one guy—"

"Enough!" Gretchen decreed sharply, getting the picture. She'd wanted to collect some memories. This one was going to be a doozy. Resigned to her fate, she dredged up her newly created alter-ego. "Okay, I'll wait here in the car, boss," she said with a forced grin. "I'll keep the motor running in case we need to make a fast getaway. Me and Rocky'll keep a sharp eye out for the fuzz."

"Cut it out, Gretchen," Michael snapped impatiently, and climbed out of the car. He leaned down and spoke through the window. "It's time to get serious. Keep the doors locked. I'll be right back."

As Gretchen watched him striding toward the office, she saw something which up until now she hadn't noticed. Michael's shoulders had a definite slump and his movements were slow. He looked tired and she instantly forgave him for snapping at her. From his point of view she supposed this was a likely place for them to stay.

The room was all she expected and more. The decor was dingy brothel with an eclectic touch of cheap Danish modern. A huge waterbed took up most of the space and Rocky immediately assumed it was his home away from home.

"Do you want to start a flood?" Michael shouted as the dog prepared to leap into the middle of the quavering velvet mattress.

"Down, Rocky," Gretchen commanded, pointing her finger to the far corner of the room where a thin rug covered the speckled linoleum floor. She followed behind her dog, pulling the French tassels on the venetian blinds and closing out the view of the street.

Michael dropped an armload of assorted tote bags and allowed the sack of dog food to slither down his legs. "I've got a headache that won't quit. We're not meeting Barney until tonight, and before then I've got to get some sleep. Do you think you can keep yourself occupied while I take a nap?"

"Yes, but what'll we do for lunch? I'm sorry, but I'm really starving." Gretchen would rather not have bothered him with something so mundane, but she didn't like the looks of the neighborhood and didn't dare go out alone. Yet, asking Michael to go with her was out of the question. He looked ready to drop. There were dark shadows under his eyes, his complexion was gray. He wasn't yet fully recovered and Gretchen's instincts told her rest was the best thing for him.

"Call room service. I think they send food over from the bar and grill next door." He dropped down on the bed. "Order something for me, too. I'll eat it when I wake up." The words were barely out of his mouth before he was asleep.

Over the next three hours Gretchen ate more preservatives than she had in the last year. Since there were no chairs in the room, she had no option but to sit on the bed. As the afternoon wore on, curiosity got the best of her and she was thankful Michael was a sound sleeper, for she gathered some amazing knowledge on human sexuality.

On the small television screen that was situated in a direct line with the bed, she learned how the Buffys, Bambis, and Lolas of the world passed their time. While working in the inner city, Gretchen had thought she couldn't be easily shocked but was proved wrong.

"Taking notes, Partridge?" Michael's curious voice interrupted her spellbound state.

A wild blush beating in her cheeks, Gretchen hastily fumbled with the remote control console built into the headboard. She was horrified when the mattress beneath them began vibrating and music blared from the speakers attached at the corners of the ceiling. As she frantically pushed more buttons, pink light flooded the room and Michael burst out laughing.

"Lord, help me!" Gretchen cried out in dismay. "How do you turn this thing off?"

"Allow me." Michael chuckled. "The Lord won't come near this place." With amazing speed, he efficiently brought the room under control.

"You've been here before," she accused, sure of it when she saw the bright color creeping up his neck. "Any man who would frequent a place like this is low, really low."

Michael cleared his throat. "It wasn't like that."

He gave the weak excuse that he'd done an exposé for his paper at a similar establishment. "Hmmph." She scowled at him. "A likely story. If I were your mother, Michael Hamilton, I'd disown you."

"She did."

His tone was so matter-of-fact, she was instantly deflated and sank limply back against the headboard. "What do you mean, she did?"

Although he rarely spoke of his childhood, Michael found himself telling Gretchen about the incorrigible he'd been as a child and youth. "I can't blame my mother. I was too much for her," he concluded. "If my dad had stuck around, things might have been different. Nowadays I think they call kids like me hyperactive, but back then I was labeled wayward. I didn't become the well-behaved gentleman you see before you now until I joined the service."

"Gentleman? That's debatable," Gretchen teased.

Michael looked offended. "I've been on my best behavior since we met."

Gretchen rolled her eyes, but this insight into his

childhood went a long way toward cementing her feelings about him. There was a lot of the lovable, if hyperactive, boy still left in the man, and she adored every vital inch of him. She'd guessed he was a hell-raiser from the beginning, but that only made him seem more exciting.

Opposites must attract. Their childhoods were as different as night and day. When she was a child the worst thing she'd ever done was steal one pack of gum from the grocery store, and she'd only been four years old at the time. Up until the day she'd discovered a big lump of a man in the swamp, she'd walked the straight and narrow.

"What's the B in your name stand for? Bold?" Gretchen smiled over at him, caught up in the image of the boy he'd once been.

"Stands for Brendan, and according to my mother, St. Brendan was bold. He was a sixth century Irish leader and my mother had high hopes. Mother Filomena told me I was a leader, but I led in the wrong direction."

"The good sister was right," Gretchen quipped. "Just look where you've led me."

"Not near as far as I plan to." He leered at her, not a trace of repentance on his handsome features.

"Oh, really?" Gretchen warmed under his gaze. A woman could get lost in those eyes, she thought, and leaned toward him, her heart swelling as his dimples beckoned to her. Her lips parted as his gaze focused on them.

With a lusty growl he dragged her down on the mattress and swept her beneath him. "No sense letting all this go to waste." He reached toward the console. The pink lights went on. He kissed the corner of her mouth and the mattress began to ripple in sensuous waves. Her giggle was cut off when his tongue sought the honeyed taste of her as soft music filled the room. The teasing atmosphere was quickly dispelled as desire took over.

He took his time undressing her, his fingertips and mouth worshiping each sensitive spot he uncovered. "This time I'm going to see what I'm touching."

Even though she had expressed her disapproval of the accoutrements of the room, Gretchen was grateful for the pink light that glowed on her naked skin. Michael's eyes were adoring, soft, and wondrous as he surveyed her breasts, narrow waist, and shapely legs.

"In the darkness of your nest you were wonderful, but in the light you're fantastic." His hand cupped one breast, his thumb pressing the dusky center. "You're beautiful, Gretchen."

She knew she wasn't, but he made her feel that way. He was the one who was truly beautiful, she decided after he'd left the bed and urgently began stripping off his clothes. Standing naked before her, his body was bathed in the soft light. It emphasized every muscle and she couldn't take her eyes off him. The solid strength of him made her shiver with awareness. He was a magnificent male and he wanted her. She opened her arms to him.

Savoring the full impact of his considerable weight bearing down on her, Gretchen curved her bare feet around his ankles. The tension within them built as he began a trail of fire down her throat and beyond. Where before he had worshiped, he now devoured, and Gretchen lost herself in the primitive mastery of his lovemaking.

"Oh, Mack," she sighed, unconsciously reverting to the name she'd called out in passion the night before.

"Not Mack," Michael negated huskily as he deliberately blew on her dampened nipples. They puckered almost painfully with the erotic action.

"Michael. Say *my* name," he ordered. "A real man is about to make love to you."

"Michael." His name came hoarsely from between her lips as his hands slipped between her legs and his mouth drew on one throbbing nipple with tantalizing possessiveness.

"Make me yours," he demanded in a ragged tone to the woman writhing beneath him. "As much as you are mine." He took her hands, encouraging them to explore his body.

Whispering his praise, he quivered at her slightest touch. His tormented breathing told her he couldn't take much more and she delighted in the gratified look on his face when she slid on top of him. Her body vibrated with desire and the erotic motions of the bed, but she wasn't yet ready to relinquish the control he'd invited her to take.

She tantalized him with the brush of her nipples on his hair-matted chest as he began pleading, "Now Gretchen, please. Take me inside you."

"Not yet," she breathed, a secretive smile playing about her lips when she noted his pained expression.

Heady with female power, she lowered her mouth to his nipples. She wanted him to remember this for as long as he lived, just as she would. He was about to discover that she could be a dangerous woman, an exciting woman, a deserving partner in this wild adventure. When her fingers closed over him, his impatience grew to explosive proportions.

"No more," he growled. The power contained in him erupted and he flipped her over on the bed, then drove inside her.

It was Michael she called out for and his name that came again and again as he accelerated their motion to a dazzling pitch. Their joining was beyond anything Gretchen could describe. With all of her strength she clung to him until they shuddered in climax.

Gretchen perused the plastic-coated menu, crinkling her nose with distaste. Every item on it was fried. She wasn't surprised. The truck stop sold quantity not quality. It looked like she had her choice between a greasy hamburger or greasy chicken and all she could eat. She chose the chicken. At least she could peel the skin off of that and conserve some calories.

As Michael ordered a double cheeseburger, onion rings, and french fries, plus a chocolate shake, he looked like he'd died and gone to heaven. "At last, real food," he sighed with contentment.

"Real food? Everything on the menu is junk food!" Gretchen denounced as soon as the waitress had left their booth. "Don't you worry about cholesterol?"

"I figure a little grease keeps the body lubricated," Michael replied in all seriousness. "Life's too short to worry about little things like that."

"Yours is going to be a whole lot shorter unless you do start worrying about it," she warned.

"You should be concerned about your own eating habits," he riposted neatly. "You need some good red meat in your diet. As far as I can tell, you don't eat anything but rabbit food. I'll take a good juicy steak any day over that gunk you eat."

Gretchen bristled with irritation. "I didn't ask you to stay and if you didn't like my food, you didn't have to eat it."

"It was the only way I could get something decent to drink," he reminded, glaring at her with riveting blue eyes.

The meaningless argument might have escalated further if the waitress hadn't returned with their meals. As Gretchen fastidiously arranged the small dishes of applesauce and coleslaw that accompanied the paper-lined basket of golden fried chicken, Michael devoured half of his cheeseburger. "What do you do, inhale those things?"

"Have to keep my strength up," he mumbled between bites. "Been getting a lot of exercise lately."

He turned his choir-boy innocence on her, but Gretchen was not amused. The glow she'd felt after their session in bed had waned considerably in the hours that had followed. They had had nothing to do but wait until their scheduled meeting with Barney Shultz, and Michael had grown more restless with each passing hour.

Rocky had been no help. Used to daily romps around the countryside, he'd become as restless as Michael and in desperate need to be taken outside. Michael had volunteered to walk him, and Gretchen had hoped that both the big lugs in her life would return in better humor. Unfortunately the reverse had been true.

Gretchen had been content to while away the time with her knitting, but Michael had nothing to occupy either his hands or his mind. He'd soon become bored with the pornographic movies, the only things shown on the television, and had begun pacing. His nervousness had transferred to the dog, and long before it was time to meet Barney, both males had been nearly climbing the walls. Michael had seemed to resent her ability to amuse herself and had begun sniping at her, an activity he had continued as they drove to the truck stop.

"Why the hell isn't Barney here yet?" Michael wiped his mouth with a paper napkin and leaned back in the booth. His eyes kept going to the door and back to the clock on the wall.

"Settle down. He's only a few minutes late. Maybe he had trouble finding this place." Gretchen's patience was gone and it was evident in her voice. "I don't know why you had to choose a place so far out of town."

"Use your head—it had to be off the beaten track," Michael growled. "We could hardly show up at the Ritz dressed in fatigues or have an attendant park Rocky."

Gretchen was willing to give him that. She wasn't dressed much better herself and their sloppy attire did fit in nicely with that of the other patrons. It was also true that Rocky's presence in the car narrowed down their choice of restaurants. "You're right," she placated. Rather than risking bearing the brunt of more of his grumbling, Gretchen concentrated on the cup of tea in front of her.

Every time the door opened, Michael tensed and Gretchen knew it was not only his impatience with the wait. Blue eyes that had been dancing with humor or darkened with desire for her were sharp with anxiety. There was a deep furrow between his brows. She didn't need for him to tell her that he was feeling exposed, fearing the worst could happen at any moment.

"Michael," she said softly as she placed her hand

over his drumming fingers. "He'll be here. You said we can trust him. He's just been detained. I know—"

"*You* don't know anything!" Michael exploded, jerking his hand out from under hers.

Gretchen felt as if he'd slapped her. Tears of frustration and hurt stung her eyes. "You're right again," she admitted in a small voice, dipping her head to avoid Michael's black scowl. "I've never been involved in anything like this. I'm not a very good moll; I really am a coward."

Bracing herself for recriminations, she blinked away the threatening tears. She jumped when Michael's fingers touched her chin and forced her up to face him. "You're not a coward, Gretchen, far from it," Michael assured with infinite compassion and tenderness. "I'm being a brute and I'm sorry."

The blue eyes that had smote her with such chilling efficiency were now soft, searching her face and reaching out to her. The pad of his thumb rubbed gently along her jawline, "Forgive me?" He brightened considerably when she nodded her head.

The mischief Gretchen found irresistible glinted in his eyes while a satisfied and very male smile eased across his lips. "You're a very good moll, Partridge," he said in a low, smooth voice. "You were everything a gangster could have wanted this afternoon."

Gretchen's cheeks burned in remembrance. If she ever wrote her memoirs about this adventure, this afternoon's activities would have to be written on asbestos. She wished she could have said something witty in return to hide her embarrassment but could do nothing but squirm uncomfortably on the cold vinyl-upholstered banquette.

"You two lovebirds mind if I join you?" a man's voice broke in and effectively cooled the flames smoldering between Gretchen and Michael.

"Barney," Michael hissed, and withdrew his hand from Gretchen. "Where the hell have you been?"

Barney Shultz dragged a chair from a nearby table and seated himself at the end of the booth. "Good to see you, buddy," he said jovially. His round face was wreathed with a broad smile, but there was no humor in his eyes.

"Act natural and friendly," he whispered so softly Gretchen barely heard him. "Can't be too careful."

Reaching for a menu propped beside the napkin holder, he pretended to be studying it. In the same low tone he informed, "Those two guys at the counter are our men. I don't recognize any of the others in here, but I'm pretty sure they're nothing more than what they seem. A few truckers, maybe a good ol' boy or two from around here."

After glancing over his shoulder and nodding his head almost imperceptibly at one of the burly, denim-jacketed men at the counter, he leaned forward, turning his full attention on Gretchen and Michael. "Listen up, I don't know how safe it is here. I wish you'd agreed to the pancake house I suggested. This place has never been checked out, but we're here so we might as well get on with it. We agents don't sculk around in the shadows any more than we have to."

Michael's impatience, never far from the surface, couldn't be contained. "What took you so long? Why weren't you here on time?"

A slight smirk turned up Barney's full lips. "I've been waiting for some information about your two cop friends." He blithely changed the subject. "By the way, hotshot, you've been under our surveillance since this afternoon. We've had this place staked out as well as that crazy motel you're staying in." He ducked his balding head but not fast enough to hide his knowing grin from Gretchen. "Why there? Though I'll admit it's an interesting place."

Gretchen wanted to slither under the table, sure the agent knew how they'd spent the afternoon. She looked to Michael, hoping he'd say something that would make the situation less embarrassing.

"I thought a no-questions-asked place was best," Michael said defensively, then quickly changed the subject. "How'd you find us?"

"We ran a make on the lady's car. It was simple to pick you up in that flashy little number, especially with that dog tucked in with you. We had you in our sights not long after you turned onto route 33."

The waitress appeared and while Barney placed an order for coffee and asked about the homemade pies offered on the menu, Michael shot Gretchen a definite "I told you so" look. There was no way she could retaliate, so Gretchen merely glared back at him, full of her own righteousness. Conversation didn't resume until after Barney's coffee and pie were delivered.

Barney leaned forward and talked in hushed tones as he toyed with the whipped cream piled on his chocolate pie.

"Grimes, Mosher, and Townsend have already been picked up, so that ends the lady's involvement. There's no reason for us to keep her under wraps." He turned to Gretchen and gave her a short smile. "I'm sorry we haven't exactly been introduced, but I guess we both know who we are. We're going to make sure you get home safely and we'll keep an agent or two around those parts for a while, but we're pretty sure you'll be okay."

"Pretty sure?" Michael questioned, barely managing to keep his voice down to an acceptable level. "That's not good enough, Barney. You'd better be damned sure nothing happens to Gretchen."

"Nothing's ever certain, you know that." He fixed Michael with a penetrating stare which was returned just as strongly. "All right, I'm as sure as I can be. Satisfied?" He waited until Michael nodded and mumbled something Gretchen couldn't hear.

Barney directed his next information to Gretchen. "We'll escort you back to the motel, if you need to pick up anything, then we'll follow you home. I assume you understand that you're not to tell anyone about any of this."

Gretchen nodded. "When do we go?"

"As soon as we leave here."

"What about Michael?" Gretchen asked quickly. "Is he free to go, too?"

Barney's mouth tightened. "That's not possible yet."

Barney's expression was so grim, Gretchen felt a return of fear, more stark and vivid than any she'd experienced throughout the past incredible thirty-six hours. She slid her hands across the table and Michael encased them in his own. His strength and warmth weren't enough to chase away the icy shroud that had settled over her. Turning stricken eyes on Barney, she asked, "Why not?"

"I'm sorry, Miss Stockwell. I'm not authorized to tell you much. We're playing this one pretty close to the chest. All I can tell you is that we think it would be best to keep Michael under tight security." Barney washed the last of his pie down with his coffee. "Let's go."

They paused only to pay the check before leaving the restaurant. Two men, whom Gretchen had noticed lounging around a huge semi when she and Michael had arrived, fell into step behind them. A frosty wind swirled around Gretchen, adding to the cold that had come over her. She shuddered and Michael reassuringly squeezed the hand he'd grabbed hold of as soon as they'd risen from the booth.

Striding briskly toward her car, he announced, "I'm going to drive Gretchen back to the motel myself."

"Sorry," Barney negated, and placed a restraining hand on Michael's shoulder. "You're going with me. We didn't see anything suspicious all day, but we can't be sure the wrong people haven't spotted you, too."

Michael swore viciously under his breath, then turned on Barney, towering several inches over the man. "Will you at least give us a few minutes? Alone."

"I can manage five minutes and that's all, but we're keeping our eyes on you."

"I guess that'll have to do." There was an exasperated edge to Michael's voice and a grim set to his features. Without another word he started toward the shadows of a huge truck parked not far from the little red Fiat. Pulling her into his arms, Michael held her close.

They stood, arms around each other, for several quiet moments. Gretchen's cheek rested against his chest. She squeezed her eyes shut, wanting to block out everything but Michael, the feel of him, his scent, the sound of his heart beating strongly and steadily.

"Gretchen?" Michael's voice fell softly against the top of her head.

She tilted her head up to look at him. He looked anguished, lost, and she offered a tentative smile of reassurance. She didn't receive the winning smile she wanted in return. Instead he studied her face as if memorizing her features.

"I don't know what to say. I . . ." He faltered, then gave a short derisive chuckle. "Hell. There isn't anything to say in this situation. I don't know where they're going to stash me, for how long, nothing. I'm positive they won't let me communicate with anybody, so don't expect to hear from me."

Gretchen nodded her head, afraid to say much for fear her voice would break. Michael didn't need that. "I . . . I understand," she said a little tremulously.

Michael felt his insides knot up. He didn't want to trust her safety to someone else. She was his partridge, his to protect, but he wasn't going to be allowed to do it. He saw the glitter of moisture in her eyes and could well imagine what was causing it. She was frightened, not for herself, but for him. "I'll be okay and so will you—once you're away from me."

Michael's last words seemed so final, so desolate, as if they held more meaning than the obvious. Was he trying to tell her she'd always be better off without him? She snuggled a little closer into his arms, searching for some way to tell him she was a better person for having spent this brief time with him, that she loved him.

Underneath the mischievous grins, twinkling eyes, the brawny exterior, lurked the rambunctious boy whom his mother couldn't handle, and though he hadn't said it, Gretchen wondered if he hadn't felt rejected by the woman. Now he was being shut away again, for his own safety, but still away from the mainstream of life, just as he'd been shut away in a strict school, shunted off to the Marines as soon as he turned eighteen.

The restrictions were going to drive him crazy. Would they be any easier for him if she told him she loved him, wanted him when he could again walk safely through the world? They'd never talked beyond the immediate moment, so Gretchen had kept her love for him a secret. She'd learned to feel again and had new courage to face emotions. She had Michael to thank for that, but she hadn't the courage to lay those emotions bare—not yet.

In the shadows Gretchen couldn't see Michael's expressive eyes. She could only hope they were relaying all the longing she was feeling. He slid his hand to her shoulders and kissed her on the forehead. "You've been great through this whole mess and I don't even know where to start thanking you."

Someone, probably Barney Shultz, cleared his throat in an unmistakable signal that their time was up. Striving for a lightheartedness she was far from feeling, Gretchen said, "You don't have to thank me. It's been an adventure we partridges don't usually get the chance to have. It's me who should be doing the thanking." Grinning pertly up at him, she cautioned him in a mock cold voice, "If you chuck me on the chin and say, 'Here's lookin' at you kid,' I'll guarantee my foot will make connections with your knee."

She pulled his face down and gave him a quick kiss, then turned away to hide her tears, but was immediately hauled back into his arms. His lips met hers, found hers unerringly, and his tongue swept through her mouth, consuming her sweetness so thoroughly Gretchen felt her knees go weak. Wrapping her arms tightly around his neck, Gretchen returned his kiss with all the hunger and longing she knew she would feel in the coming weeks . . . months . . . perhaps forever.

9

Gretchen tucked another pillow behind her patient's head. "There, Mr. Eldridge." She smiled warmly at the elderly man's thin, lined face. "Is that more comfortable?"

"You goin' to put the squeeze on my arm again?" Eldridge asked with a noticeable twinkle in his pale blue eyes.

"Sure am," Gretchen answered, grinning as she wrapped the pressure cuff in place and squeezed the inflation bulb.

Watching the guage carefully, she concentrated on the beats registering on the manometer, then released the cuff. Shaking her head from side to side, she remarked brightly, "A little high but not too bad. You better stop chasing the nurses for a couple of days, though."

"Can't do that, I'd die for sure. You're just sorry I don't chase after you," Eldridge teased. "You'll have to wait some and get a little experience and a mite more meat on you afore I'm interested. You're just not ready for a man like me," he continued, hoping to bring a blush to Gretchen's cheeks.

"Now, you take a woman like Miz Huffmeyer." Eldridge winked at Gretchen as he referred to the head nurse on the night shift. "There's a woman fer ya. Old enough and experienced and ripe." He reached for the newspaper, gave it a frowning glance, then tossed it aside.

"You'd better not let Mr. Huffmeyer hear you," Gretchen warned and patted the man's thin shoulder. She made the proper notations on his chart, then handed him his evening's medication. "Drink it all, Mr. Eldridge. I don't want to have to sit on you again."

He hesitated before downing the contents of the small paper cup. "If I drink it all will you read me the paper?"

"Sounds like blackmail to me, fella." She crossed her arms and tapped her toe, throwing him a stern look before softening. "I've got time to scan the headlines for you before I finish my rounds. If I can, I'll come back later and read some more to you."

She picked up the paper and started to unfold it to the front page, more eager than her patient to scan the evening edition's top stories. The trial had been going on for weeks, but so far there'd been no mention of Michael as a witness. "I'm surprised you didn't ask one of the Gray Ladies to read to you before they all left. That's what they're here for. To help out."

"Gray Ladies, Schmay Ladies," he muttered disgustedly. "All them fool women want to do is rearrange my flowers and water the plants. Don't know the first thing about takin' care of sick people."

"Now, now, Mr. Eldridge." Gretchen listened with only half an ear as she perused the headlines, looking for something, anything that related to the drug case involving Michael. Mr. Eldridge's voice droned on in the background while he listed his complaints against the hospital volunteers. Gretchen knew he really didn't mean a word of it, as he often talked about them in glowing terms. This evening he was merely using them as a scapegoat.

The man was past ninety and his body was suffering from a variety of ailments that could be very unscientifically lumped together and labeled "worn out." It was extremely frustrating to a man who'd been so active and independent all of his life to have to depend on others for some of life's most basic tasks. His tired blue eyes were clouded with inoperable cataracts and he was unable to read. That bothered him the most. He could not longer indulge in the simple pleasure of reading the newspaper, a lifelong habit.

"Well, you goin' to read my paper to me or keep all the news to yourself?" Eldridge cut in testily.

"Sorry, Mr. Eldridge," Gretchen apologized with a slight flush of color. She didn't want him to know he hadn't been receiving her full attention. At the first of the year, when she'd taken the job at the Valley Medical Center, she'd vowed her patients would receive the best care she could give them. Care. As she saw it now, that was the most important part of her work, genuinely caring for her patients and letting them know that she did.

The majority of the patients in her ward were elderly

and many had few visitors. Their families and friends had either preceded them in death or were far too weak to make frequent visits. These people needed warmth and mindful attendance even more than the medical treatment they were receiving. Far too many of them were spending their final days in the center, and the staff tried to make it as loving an atmosphere as possible.

Gretchen read the front page headlines, looked up at the clock, and decided she could spend a few more minutes. There wasn't anything on the front page about the trial, but then, she hadn't really expected it. It was no longer a hot story and was relegated farther back in the paper.

"Not too much different here. The president's appointment of Garland Newcomb to the Cabinet has been approved by Congress and the Senate. Nothing too startling about that," she editorialized. "We all knew he'd be approved, didn't we, Mr. Eldridge?" Getting a conferring nod from her listener, she turned to the next page. "Let's see what else there is to offer."

Using an anchorman's tone, she began. "On the statewide scene the governor has appointed a special committee to look into the secondary schools' graduation requirements. Let's see," she went on. "They're picketing a steel mill near Akron. The weather will continue to be cold with intermittant flurries all week."

She scanned the page and the next, looking for something to interest Mr. Eldridge that wasn't a repeat of the previous day's news. Her gaze swung down the page, then quickly refocused on the center. Michael's face was glowering back at her.

She blinked, thinking it might be a mirage, but he was still there when she opened her eyes. Dark curls fell across a broad forehead, a wide firm mouth cut a line above a square chin. The picture was in black and white, of course, but Gretchen knew the color of his eyes. They were blue, a rich cobalt blue, where sparkles of humor could appear without warning. She began reading the accompanying article, her heart thumping so strongly she was sure her blood pressure must be matching Mr. Eldridge's.

"Find something interesting? Come on, don't keep it to yourself." Mr. Eldridge prodded her to read the article aloud.

"Ah . . . 'The state produced their star witness today in the trial involving more than two dozen defendants accused of trafficking illegal drugs over a tristate area. Michael B. Hamilton, a reporter for this paper, has been kept under protective custody by the F.D.A. until his appearance today. Hamilton testified that—"

"Didn't I tell you the G-men had something up their sleeve in that case?" Eldridge cut in with a grin of satisfaction. "You're probably too young to remember a TV show called *The Untouchables,* but it used to be my favorite."

The mention of illegal trafficking must have touched off memories, for Mr. Eldridge began to reminisce about "the old days" when rumrunners and stills were rampant in the hill country. He rambled a while about "Hoover's boys," seemingly unaware that J. Edgar Hoover was no longer alive and the present drug case was being handled more by the F.D.A. than the F.B.I. Stilling her curiosity to read further, Gretchen listened patiently until abruptly, Mr. Eldridge announced that he was sleepy and bid her good night.

Gretchen completed her rounds with some difficulty, forcing herself to keep her mind on her work and not on the newspaper resting innocuously at the nurse's station. She'd just returned when a blinking red light on the monitoring screen obliterated all thoughts but the middle-aged heart patient going into cardiac arrest. Gretchen spent her last hour of duty assisting a doctor in fighting for the woman's life. They won the battle and Gretchen stayed another hour to complete the necessary paperwork after an air-vac helicopter had whisked the patient off to Columbus for more extensive treatment.

Exhausted, Gretchen drove the few miles to her home. A copy of the *Columbus Sentinel* was folded beneath her purse. She'd been forced to delay reading it for a few hours already and decided that delaying a little longer wouldn't make much difference. She wanted to be alone when she finished it.

Rocky greeted her enthusiastically when she stepped inside the back door. "You won't settle down until you get your loving for the day, will you?" she cooed to the dog as she tossed the paper on the table and bent to wrap her arms around the animal's muscular neck.

She straightened and gave him a final pat, and Rocky, content with having received his requested ration of affection, whined and gazed longingly at the door. "Don't be gone too long," she called after him as he disappeared through the doorway and into the darkness beyond her back step.

After starting the fire in the cook stove and placing the kettle on to heat some water for tea, Gretchen settled herself at the table. The newspaper lay inches from her fingertips, but she hesitated picking it up. At the hospital she'd been eager to read the report of the trial, but now? Now she feared the disappointment that might result.

If Michael were freed from protective custody, was

there any assurance that he would seek her out? Maybe it was better not to know, not to get her hopes up. She'd been so excited when the trial had finally started. However, with each passing week with no word from Michael, she'd become less eager to read about it. Her doubts concerning their ever having a relationship increased. After all, what did one really know about a person after that short length of time?

"You're just being a coward!" Gretchen condemned herself aloud and forced herself to reach for the newspaper. The teakettle whistled its readiness, and Gretchen felt as if she'd been granted a reprieve. She dropped the paper and crossed the kitchen to lift the kettle from the stove. Methodically she tossed a teabag into a cup, poured in the water, and retraced her steps.

The paper still wasn't open to the appropriate page. Gretchen sipped her tea, staring at the bold headlines announcing the official appointment of Garland Newcomb as Secretary of State. "Good choice, Mr. President."

Scowling, she placed her cup into the saucer with a clatter. "You're stalling again, Gretchen Stockwell."

With unsteady hands she opened the paper and laid it out on the table. Michael still stared at her from the center of page three. Studying the picture, she frowned. There was no mistaking Michael, even without the caption beneath the picture. He looked tired, perhaps a little thinner, but the resolution wasn't very sharp, so maybe the photo was deceiving.

Tearing her hungry gaze from the picture, she gathered her courage and read the lead paragraph. Because of Michael's testimony, Duard Clinton, owner of a chain of fitness clubs, was expected to be found guilty of all charges made against him. The prosecution and the defense would be offering their final summations the next day, and then it would be up to the jury. The details of Michael's testimony were given in the following paragraph.

Gretchen paused and put down the paper, noting for the first time that it was a day old. She'd worked a double shift and been so busy, she hadn't paid any attention to the latest news until Mr. Eldridge had requested she read to him. Suddenly, frantic to know what had happened during the previous day, she flipped on the radio, trying to find something other than music, but in vain. She'd have to wait until the hour for any kind of news report.

Because of the Mack Dawson series, Michael had obviously been suspected of knowing about Clinton's involvement. That was the reason why he'd been kept under such tight security. The F.D.A. had feared men like Grimes and Mosher might make another attempt on Michael's life. Mack Dawson's suspicion of the owner of a fictional tennis club had been too close to the truth for an actual illegal operation's comfort.

As Gretchen finished reading the article, she felt more chilled with each word of Michael's statement. The details of the attempt on his life and the revelations his two assailants had made when they'd been looking for what they'd hoped was his body horrified her. She squeezed her eyes shut remembering the salvo of shots she'd heard that morning and the unconscious man she'd found beside the swamp. They'd come so close, so close to killing him and if they had she wouldn't have met the most exciting man who'd ever walked into her life.

But now, months had gone by since she'd seen Michael. Months since she'd stood in his arms in a

windswept parking lot outside a truck stop. Her fingertips rose to brush her lips. Michael had been in and out
of her life so quickly yet the memory of his kisses, his
tender lovemaking, that devilish smile hadn't faded.

She gave herself a little shake, coming back to the
present. There was nothing in the article to indicate
whether Michael was free to go or would remain under
F.D.A. protection until the end of the trial. Would that
mean another delay in their reunion? Who was she
kidding? Perhaps there never would be a reunion.
There had been no promises made, no plans for seeing
each other again once the ordeal was over.

Staring at the picture of Michael, Gretchen gave
herself another mental shake. It was ridiculous to sit
around waiting for a call or a visit that might never
come. Their relationship had been intense but of short
duration, an exciting fantasy come true. They'd been
caught up in an incredible situation. Maybe that had
been the only reason for their attraction, an attraction
that could very well be as brief and crazy as the
circumstances that had prompted it.

During the first week after her return to the cabin,
Gretchen had tried to put the whole thing behind her,
treasure it as a fond memory, and step back into her
normal routine. However, that had proved impossible.
Knowing Michael, even for such a brief time, had
changed her. Loving Michael was as spontaneous and
irresistible as the man himself.

During the Christmas holidays she'd flown to Arizona
to spend a few days with her parents. After her father's
retirement, they'd purchased a new home in Phoenix.
Architecturally, the house was radically different from
the more formal structure they'd occupied in Shaker

Heights, but the atmosphere inside was the same, far too sterile and controlled for Gretchen's taste. Even so, she'd been glad to see her parents and for the most part, the visit was a happy one. However, she'd been eager to return to the rustic little cabin she called home, rapidly tiring of her parents' continual suggestions that she move back to civilization.

"Gretchen, you're different," her mother had said over breakfast one morning. "You've got more sparkle than I've seen in you since you were a little girl. What's happened to you?"

Gretchen had nearly choked on her croissant. Looking across the glass-topped table at her regal mother, Gretchen had been tempted to say, "I had a brief wild fling as a gangster's moll, Mom. It was the most exciting thing in the world and I'll never be the same."

That would surely have shaken her mother's cool demeanor, but Gretchen had thought better of it. Instead, she'd merely responded with a noncommital, "I'm very haapy in my new life."

It was true. Because of Michael, she'd stepped back into the mainstream of living. The cabin was still her home and weaving still occupied many hours of each week, but she'd made an effort to come out of herself, meet people, and become part of the community. Even more important than the new friendships she had formed was how she felt about herself.

She no longer felt defeated by life but embraced it. Gretchen wasn't surprised that her mother had noticed something different about her. With a touch of sadness, she wondered if either of her parents would possibly understand if she tried to explain it. She doubted it.

It was easier to let them believe that the only thing she

was excited about was starting in the nursing position she'd accepted. She did like her job. In the small hospital just outside of Lancaster, she had reentered the medical world she'd been part of before, but this time with a whole heart.

She still loved her cabin but didn't hole up in it anymore. It was a retreat—or a nest, as Michael would have called it—but one she now felt free to leave. She enjoyed going out even though her activities seemed bland when compared to those days she'd spent with Michael. Most of her new friends were married, but there were a few single ones, some of whom were male. She'd even accepted a few dates but kept the relationships platonic.

For the present there was only one man whose smile could make her melt, whose laughter enticed her to join him in merriment, and whose kisses turned her knees to water. That man was still being held a virtual prisoner somewhere safe. Until he was free and she knew for certain whether there was any future for them, she was as much a prisoner as he was. She could physically come and go but her willingness to open herself to a relationship with any other man was securely locked away.

The agent that had escorted Gretchen back to the motel that cold November night hadn't been any more forthcoming with information than Barney Shultz. The only thing she could get out of him was that Michael would be very safe and that she shouldn't try to contact him through Barney. Any communication she might make to the F.D.A. agents could jeopardize her safety and Michael's as well as the case. She didn't even know if he was in the state.

There'd been times she'd wanted to scream with frustration, yell at somebody, but then she'd thought of Michael. At least she was free to come and go as she liked. There were no restrictions as there were on him. Knowing him, that must be driving him crazy.

Michael was a man of action and she knew throughout his enforced incarceration, he had vented some of his pent-up energy at the typewriter. His column, "The City Talks," had continued without interruption, as had the Mack Dawson series. Gretchen saw them as her only means of communication with Michael and she'd read them over and over again.

At first there had been nothing extraordinary in the series, but then subtly the main character and the story line had changed. Hard-nosed Mack Dawson developed an interest in a woman, one woman, and softened his macho attitude toward the entire female population. The woman, Molly Stecker, was described as a golden-eyed, golden-haired beauty, voluptuous, very sexy, and glamorous. Since the series appeared in a newspaper, Mack and Molly's relationship was implied rather than described in detail. However, there was no doubt that the relationship was very passionate.

At first Gretchen didn't see herself as an inspiration for the character. It wasn't until Molly's boudoir was described that Gretchen began to suspect something and her mortification began to build. She knew writers often used their own experiences in their stories, but if she ever saw Michael again she vowed she'd hit him with something for describing Molly's bedroom the way that he had.

The voluptuous Molly lived in a penthouse that was a far cry from Gretchen's very earthbound cabin but for her bedroom . . . That had been described in the segment that had appeared only two weeks ago. Gretchen had read it so many times she had it memorized.

I leaned my shoulder against the doorframe as I took the measure of the room. It was like nothing I'd ever seen and I'd seen a lot of bedrooms. This one was a combination of the *Arabian Nights* and the *Swiss Family Robinson.*

"Come on in, Big Daddy," Molly invited with a promising huskiness in her voice. "Make yourself right at home."

She patted the red velvet bedspread and the mattress came alive. It undulated like the ocean on a calm day. The frame was massive tree trunks, probably teak, as Molly's taste seemed to lean toward the exotic. A canopy of woven bamboo hid the pink light bulbs that glowed from the corners, and music was being piped in from speakers hidden somewhere in the mirrored ceiling.

I knew Molly was offering me much more than a place to sleep for the night. Somehow I sensed I'd be spending more than one night with her. Molly wasn't the kind of woman a man could forget.

We came together like twin flames and in her seductive eyes I caught a glimpse of what the future could be like for me if I played my cards right. "Today, you're my woman, sweetheart," I muttered as I grabbed a handful of her silky hair. "But what about tomorrow?"

"Tomorrow?" she whispered back, a mysterious smile playing about her generous red lips. "We'll just have to see, Mack, darling. We'll just have to see."

* * *

Gretchen knew what had inspired the bedroom depicted in Michael's story, but Molly Stecker? No, Gretchen didn't think she'd inspired the sultry blonde with the exotic penthouse. She had nothing in common with that woman at all. Had Michael once been involved with a woman like that? Was he still? If so, she didn't have a chance of holding his interest.

Michael's knowledge of the console above the bed at the Twin Hills and his embarrassment when she'd called him to it made Gretchen wonder just what kind of story he'd been researching when he'd admitted to having been in that sort of establishment before. Had he shared a similar room with someone other than Gretchen? Someone more like this Molly?

As the story went on, Gretchen found herself growing increasingly jealous. Envying a fictional character was ridiculous and she knew it, but she couldn't help herself. She was probably the only fan of the Mack Dawson series who wasn't hoping for Mack and Molly to get together at the end.

The only real pleasure she got from reading the serial was that it seemed proof that Michael was safe somewhere. He couldn't have completed the entire story before the strange odyssey they had shared or he wouldn't have been able to describe that bed. Also, Mack Dawson had started using more caution, thinking more about the future. If knowing Michael had made a difference in her life and the way she looked at things, couldn't the reverse be true?

Did Michael Hamilton now think before acting, think of a future with one woman? Was that woman her or somebody else? Gretchen didn't know where Michael was being kept or under what conditions. Maybe a female agent had been assigned to guard him and maybe she was the inspiration for Molly.

Mack Dawson's case was winding to a close. The teaser at the end of last Sunday's installment had been, "Find out next week how Mack cracks the case. Who is 'Mr. Big,' and will Mack find his beautiful Molly?"

"These and the answers to other burning questions will be revealed in next week's paper," Gretchen mocked in a deep voice as she went to answer Rocky's scratching summons at the door. There were several "burning questions" she wanted answered, too, and they weren't centered on Mack but his creator.

After her simple dinner Gretchen settled herself before the loom. It didn't occupy her mind totally anymore, but it did keep her hands busy. She discovered she turned the television on much more often than she once had and knew the reason why. The cabin seemed far too quiet without it. She was no longer content to weave with nothing but the quiet country sounds accompanying the thud of the beater and the soft whoosh of the shuttle. This was one of the negative results of having known Michael Hamilton. With him gone, everything around her seemed so dull.

The television was on but Gretchen wasn't paying too much attention to the sitcom being played out across the screen. She was more interested in the final news program of the day. The radio newscasts had been too brief, relating nothing more about the trial than that the jury would be bringing in a verdict at any time. There had been no details of the day's proceedings except that the summations had been made by both sides.

However, the television station hoped to provide live interviews with some of the principals of the day's court action later in the evening. Both attorneys would be consulted, as well as the state's star witness, if the latter were available for comment. "Full details will follow on the eleven o'clock news," she heard a voice announce, and she quickly gave the television her full attention.

She was too late, the regularly scheduled program was back in progress. The hands on the coach clock resting on the mantel moved slowly. Gretchen tried to concentrate on her weaving, the program, anything but the sluggish passage of time.

At last the Columbus final news program was on. After a quick review of the national scene and a commercial, the part Gretchen was waiting for began. In a corridor of the courthouse, a horde of reporters swarmed around two men whom Gretchen recognized as the attorneys for the case. She scanned the crowd eagerly, searching for a familiar curly head. She didn't see Michael but she did see Barney Shultz's bald pate shining in the crowd and so did the members of the press.

After the attorneys brushed off questions and disappeared down the hallway, Barney was cornered. Microphones from all the stations were thrust in his face. He looked tired but happy.

"Do you expect Clinton to be found guilty?"

"Any indication when the jury will bring in a verdict?"

"You had Hamilton under tight security before and during the trial. Do you expect any threats on his life now that he's given his testimony?"

Gretchen was already on the edge of her seat, but that last question brought her up to her feet. "Come on, Barney. Answer the questions. Answer all of them. Please." She didn't even realize she was pleading with the television.

"Please, it's been a long day and it might not be over yet," Barney beseeched the fast-talking crowd gathered around him. "As far as a guilty verdict, of course we want that. We've worked months on this case and we don't want it to go down the drain at this point. I don't have any more idea than you how long it'll be before the jury comes back in. It could take all night and part of tomorrow. Your guess is as good as mine."

Barney mopped his face with a crumpled handkerchief and tried to move away. Having been thwarted by the legal representation for each side, the reporters were tenacious in holding on to Barney. "Tell us about Hamilton. Are you still worried about someone trying to kill him?"

Gretchen had inched away from the television during the first part of his interview but leaned closer to hear Barney's next answer.

"We don't expect any kind of attempt on Michael Hamilton. There would be no point now. He's free to resume his life."

More questions were hurled at Barney, but Gretchen didn't listen to any more. She sat stunned for a few seconds, then jumped to her feet, letting out a victory whoop. "It's over, Rocky! The waiting is over!"

Rocky sprang to his feet and started barking as Gretchen did a little dance in the middle of the room. Not content with that, she skipped through the entire cabin with Rocky at her heels. They might have gone on dancing for hours if the telephone hadn't started ringing.

"Michael!"

10

Deep in the woods, Gretchen tramped between the melting patches of snow. As evening approached she knew she should start back to her cabin, but after weeks of being cooped up it felt good to be outdoors again. "I think winter's on its way out, don't you, boy?"

Rocky pranced along beside her, his large paws leaving prints in the slushy snow and mud. Here and there the tender shoots of spring's earliest wildflowers were pushing through the wet forest floor. The trees were still barren but Gretchen knew it would just take a week of warmer weather to bring out the buds. The snowfall of two days ago had been very wet, typical of March, and seemed to be winter's last frosty gasp before giving way to spring.

Knowing it would be less muddy to stay on the higher ground, Gretchen kept away from the swamp. She knew that wasn't her only reason for avoiding that area. She'd purposely stayed away ever since Michael.

At first it had been far too cold and the snow was too deep to venture down the steep slope to explore the marshes. Today she could excuse herself again because the ground was so soft and she might lose her way in the gathering dusk.

It was too painful to recall that day. It wasn't finding him in such a dangerously weak state that hurt to remember, but her own foolhardiness after his recovery.

Besides, there's nothing interesting around that swamp, Gretchen defended. Nothing but animal tracks that were fun to try to identify and perhaps follow for a while. Nothing but the finest place in the area to watch birds. Nothing but the best source of cattails and marsh yarrow to use for natural dyes. It wasn't a fascinating place at all, unless you enjoyed those kinds of activities —and Gretchen did.

"Damn!" The word was spoken so loudly and vehemently that Rocky immediately sat down as if he had been commanded to do so. The animal's expression was repentant. Apparently he thought he was being chastised for some wrongdoing.

"Got a guilty conscience, fella?" Gretchen asked, but patted his head and scratched behind his ears. "Sorry," she apologized. "I'm not mad at you. You're a good boy. I'm angry with myself."

Satisfied, Rocky came back on his feet and trotted along beside her. "And with good reason," Gretchen continued aloud for her audience, the quiet forest and a giant of a dog. "I can't even blame this on Michael."

There, she'd said his name, something she'd tried not

to do for more than a week. She was never going to see him again, his silence had made that perfectly clear, but it hurt, really hurt. With an impetuousness that was foreign to her nature, she'd completely lost her head and fallen in love with a man she knew hardly anything about. Moreover, he obviously didn't feel the same way about her.

"I assumed too much." She paused and absently tugged on a dead vine winding around a tree. "I was so sure he'd call or come as soon as he was freed."

She remembered the phone call she'd taken the night she'd heard that the trial was over. What a fool she'd been to think that Michael would rush to the nearest phone and call her. The person who had received her excited greeting hadn't been Michael but a nurse at the hospital asking to switch their days off. Gretchen had agreed, then quickly terminated the conversation, still hoping Michael would try to get in touch with her. She'd spent the night by a phone that had never rung.

"Damn the man!"

"Who're you swearing at, Partridge?"

Out of the shadows stepped a tall, painfully familiar figure. "Me?" Michael asked in the well-remembered tone that instantly obstructed the flow of air in Gretchen's throat.

She didn't move, couldn't have even if she'd tried, but stood gaping at him as if she'd conjured him up out of her imagination. If she had, she'd certainly dredged up an original rendition. This figment of her longing looked little like the man she'd left behind at a truck stop.

He was dressed like a conservative businessman in a wool topcoat worn over a dark three-piece suit. In the eerie light she couldn't discern the suit's color, but his white collar and the silver stripe in his tie glowed almost incandescently.

Gretchen blinked and blinked again, but the image was still there and coming closer. "Michael?" she croaked.

"Old Dimple Cheeks, himself," he said with a chuckle as he reached for her.

His head descended as he enveloped her in his arms, his mouth settling softly over hers. Because she had yearned for this moment, dreamed of it for months, Gretchen didn't question his unexpected arrival or his right to take up where they had left off. His taste was one she had craved for so long that she greedily took her fill, surprising him with the urgency of her response.

Her fingers ached for the feel of chestnut curls and she felt the sigh that left his chest as she wove her fingers into his hair. He might not be dressed the same, but he smelled the same, felt the same, and kissed the same. There was no need to reacquaint themselves, for it was as if their embrace was a continuation of the last one they had shared.

As she had then, Gretchen tried to express her longing, her desperation for his touch, his kisses, and Michael satisfied her need. He devoured the softness of her mouth, his tongue urgently appeasing her hunger even as hers provided equal sustenance. She had not yet had her fill when he shuddered and set her away from him.

His breathing was ragged, his blue eyes darker than sapphires. "Thank God," he forced out hoarsely. "What a relief."

"Relief?" Gretchen was having a similarly difficult

time controlling her own erratic breathing and much more. She'd spent every minute of the last week trying to get over him and within seconds after seeing him again, she'd been shown what a fruitless endeavor it had been. She was not only confused but angry with herself.

The man had an effect on her that just wasn't fair. She was a practical person, a logical one, but he could destroy all logic with one touch. The feelings he brought out in her weren't even civilized, and she was, above all else, a civilized person. There were hundreds of things she wanted to say to him, ask him, but after one kiss, she couldn't form a coherant thought.

In the moments that Gretchen tried, with little success, to reassemble her truant senses, Michael came to grips with his own. Keeping one arm around her waist, he started them back toward her cabin.

"I hoped you'd react this way when you saw me again, but I certainly had my doubts. All the way out here I worried whether or not you'd slam the door in my face. When you weren't in the cabin, I was afraid you'd gone out for the evening and I'd have to sit outside on your doorstep till you got home."

Gretchen finally found her voice. "You could have called first," she reproved, bitterly, cutting off her sentence before she expressed the rest of the thought— *and it should have been a lot sooner than today.*

"I didn't want to waste any time," he said, the undaunted optimism in his voice telling her the man had not changed a wit. He still behaved as if whatever he did demanded no explanation. Oblivious to the exasperation gathering force in Gretchen's hazel eyes, he went on blithely, "I wanted to get here as quickly as possible."

"I could tell," she quipped, but Michael was impervious to the sarcasm.

"I've missed you so much I've thought of nothing else but making love to you again and I knew you'd be just as impatient."

Gretchen remained silent. She was impatient, all right, but not for the same reasons he was. She wanted to hear his reasons for waiting a week to show up. While she'd been agonizing over having assumed too much, it appeared he had also—but their assumptions were miles apart. Furthermore, subtlety was not one of his strong suits. Gretchen's outrage began to build as Michael began digging a hole for himself.

"Hearing Rocky barking out in the woods was the sweetest sound I've ever heard. I knew you wouldn't go off anywhere and leave him outside, knew I'd find you out here, thinking about me."

The hole got deeper as Michael applied himself to the task in earnest.

"I was hoping I'd find my little partridge keeping the nest warm for me, but this was the next best thing. I couldn't have asked for a nicer welcome."

The hole became a huge, bottomless pit filled with the burning acid of her rage as Michael jumped in with both feet.

"Stop dragging your heels, Partridge. If we don't hurry, we'll have to get down to business right here in the woods."

Gretchen was sure that smoke was coming out of her ears and if he didn't see it, the big lug was not only dumb but blind. If she weren't a civilized human being she would have been frothing at the mouth. As it was, she could barely contain the growls trying to get past her clenched teeth. How wonderful it would be if she could forget everything and just attack. When sufficiently provoked, even the most timid of creatures turned vicious. If she were really a partridge, she'd peck him to death and leave him as carrion for the vultures.

She wrenched away from his grasp. Planting her feet firmly on the ground, she placed her hands on her hips and started in. "You . . . you . . . you . . . !"

Carried away by a rage that left her speechless, Gretchen's anger was a terrible thing to behold. Michael, over six feet tall, outweighing her by a hundred pounds, took a defensive step backward. "Something wrong?" he asked tentatively.

"Wrong? How dare you!"

Once Gretchen let loose, Michael was helpless to stop her. When he reached one hand toward her shoulder, she knocked it away. "Don't touch me! We're not caught up in a life and death situation anymore. I'm not playing the willing moll for you now!"

"But, Partridge, I—"

"That's another thing. I'm not a little brown bird! I'm a woman!"

Michael threw her his best placating smile. "Believe me, I know—"

"You don't know anything! You think you can just drop in here any old time you feel like it and I'll hop in bed with you? Ha!" She started marching toward her cabin, mimicking his words under her breath. "I just couldn't wait to get here. Kept the nest warm. Knew you'd be as impatient as I am."

She was yards beyond where she'd left him standing with a stupified look on his face. Whirling around, she shouted back, "If you were so impatient, what took you so long?"

Michael's perplexed look gave way to understanding

and his smile broadened. "You *were* impatient for me to get here, weren't you?" It wasn't a question but a statement. He started walking toward her, his confidence evident in each jaunty step.

Gretchen wasn't about to admit that she'd been dying to see him. "Hardly," she answered harshly. "You were part of a very brief adventure and I've given it *and* you very little thought."

"Oh, sure, Gretchen," Michael agreed in an indulgent tone. "I could tell by the way you kissed me that you'd forgotten all about me. There was something about the way you melted so completely into my arms that made me realize you hadn't remembered me at all." His blue eyes twinkled with merriment as he came to a halt in front of her.

"I did not," she sputtered indignantly. "You took me by surprise."

Looking down at her outraged face, Michael couldn't contain himself. With unadulterated devilment, he said, "Sweetheart, if that's how you react when you're surprised, I can't wait for your reaction when you're ready for me."

Gretchen couldn't believe her ears. She'd known he was ungovernable but this was going too far. He was so infuriatingly cocksure of himself. "You . . . you are the—"

"Man you love," he finished for her, leaning forward until his face was inches from hers. In a lower, huskier tone, he completed his statement, "And the one who loves you."

Fury gave way to shock but not completely. Those may have been the words Gretchen had yearned for, but she wasn't yet appeased. Intuitively she knew that if she didn't retain her unyielding attitude for a little while longer, he'd have her dancing on the end of puppet strings for the rest of her life.

"How can you say that?" Gretchen asked, trying to keep her voice harsh. "We hardly know each other." She folded her arms across her breasts hoping her defiant body language would convey her resistance even better than words.

"We didn't spend much time together, that's true, but I think we learned a lot about each other." Michael ignored the messages she was trying to send out and placed his hands on her shoulders, turning her gently back in the direction of the cabin. Giving her a little shove, he got her moving. He remained behind her, his hands still on her shoulders urging her forward.

He continued in a matter-of-fact manner. "I had more than two months with little to do but analyze you and how I felt about you. At first I thought you'd just let yourself get caught up in the moment, but then the more I thought about it I realized that wasn't your style. You're not the kind of woman to give yourself that freely and uninhibitedly because you got carried away. Normally I think you're a pretty cautious sort."

His voice was rumbling from just over Gretchen's shoulder and the vibrations against her neck was sending shivers of awareness down her spine. It was discomfiting to hear him announce that she loved him, even if he were professing to love her. He was far too adept at seeing through to her innermost thoughts and taking advantage of the knowledge. "There's nothing wrong with caution," she said in a weak voice, feeling the need to defend herself.

"I agree." He let loose of her shoulders long enough

to open the back door of her cabin, then pushed her inside. "In the future you'll have to be cautious enough for the both of us, I'm afraid."

Keeping her voice deceptively calm, Gretchen announced, "I'm exercising that caution right now." She pointed to one of the kitchen chairs. "Sit down!"

Feeling a strange sense of *déjà vu,* Michael did as he was told, thankful that this time he hadn't been ordered to the rickety ladderback chair in the living area. The oak mate's chair offered a far more secure resting spot for his weight.

Gretchen methodically removed her woolen poncho and hung it on one of the pegs. "First, I'm not aware there is a *both* of us nor am I aware that *we* have a future. I want to know why you think you can waltz back in here, claim to have come as soon as possible, when I know full well that you've been freed from custody for more than a week. Hocking Valley is only a little more than an hour's drive from Columbus. It wouldn't have taken you that long even if you'd walked, or are you going to claim they had you stashed away in China? I want some straight talk from you." She smacked the table top with the palm of her hand. "And right now!"

"I really do love you, you know."

"So you said, but you're not going to worm your way out of this with sweet talk. I've got your number, Michael Hamilton."

Even though her words were sharp, there was a definite thawing in her demeanor and Michael took courage. For a few brief moments he'd been afraid he'd misjudged Gretchen, that he'd offered his heart to a woman who was throwing it back to him. "I wasn't in

China. They stashed me just north of the city. I honestly haven't had time to come, because I had to fly to New York."

"New York? What were you doing there? Cavorting with Molly?" She leaned against the edge of the counter keeping a good yard or more between them. It was so good to see him, hear his voice, that it was taking every ounce of willpower she had not to leap into his arms, but she refused to do that until she got some answers.

"Molly who?" Michael looked blank.

"Molly Stecker. That sultry blonde with the exotic penthouse!"

Michael's laughter bubbled up inside him. "You're Molly, Gretchen. You had to know that. Who else would sleep in a bed like that?"

"Who are you trying to kid? That bed was operated by remote control and I know an expert was pushing the buttons. It was just as I thought, you've been in that kind of place before and it wasn't with me."

To Gretchen's increasing chagrin, Michael looked more than pleased with himself. "Jealous? This gets better and better, Partridge. I was using Molly to communicate with you, but I never expected she'd have this kind of an effect. You're jealous of yourself."

"I'm nothing like that blonde bombshell," Gretchen declared irately.

Michael leaned back in his chair and folded his arms over his chest, his blue eyes sliding hotly down her figure. "Bombshells are in the eyes of the beholder and I'm looking at one right now." He lapsed into the gangster jargon she had never thought to hear again. "Doll, you've got gams that don't quit. Your headlights are always on, making my fingers itch to hold 'em.

You've got the sweetest little body this side of south Chicago, Moll, and this Big Daddy can't wait to have it again."

The look he gave her was as unprintable as the words. Gretchen was sure the temperature in the cabin had gone up a thousand degrees. She unbuttoned the top button of her blouse to gain some relief from the wave of heat curling up from her toes. When she didn't say anything, Michael gave her a knowing smile and grinned. "Convinced?"

He saw by her flushed face that she was. "Now, then, let's get back to less interesting matters. The reason I went to New York was to meet with a publisher. They want to print as many Mack Dawson stories as I can write. We've got a lot to celebrate." He couldn't contain his excitement about the book contract he'd just signed, and started to get up off the chair.

"Oh, no, you don't. Stay where you are," she ordered sternly, regaining her composure. She'd learned her lessons well where this man was concerned. Let him wiggle off the hook for even a second and he'd swim away.

"Congratulations on the publishing of your story," she offered blandly, keeping her own reaction to the news under tight control. She would far rather have joined him in celebrating this news but decided that if—and it was a big if—he had a reasonable explanation for his silence, she'd help him celebrate later. "I'll believe that you might not have had time to come but you surely had enough time to call. There is telephone service down here you know."

Reluctantly settling back in the chair, Michael shifted his legs, a guilty expression dulling the bright highlights that had been sparkling in his eyes. "I . . . ah . . . was afraid to."

"Afraid? You afraid? You'll have to do better than that," she declared. "Afraid implies that you actually gave something a little forethought—something you never do! Afraid, my foot," she muttered.

"I was afraid of you," Michael admitted in a voice so low Gretchen wasn't sure she'd heard him right. Before she could respond he rushed on. "Afraid you wouldn't feel the same way about me. Don't you see? I had to be here, see your reaction to me. I couldn't do that over the phone.

"I love you so much but I was terrified I'd only been living out a fantasy. I didn't know if you loved me or Mack Dawson. I feel as much like Mack as you feel like Molly. You were jealous of her, well, I was just as jealous of him. Compared to that guy, I'm ordinary. Can't you see how hard it was for me thinking I was a victim of my own creation?"

There was no sign of the human dynamo in Michael's slumped figure. Gretchen did understand—very well— and her heart went out to him. He might not think so, but there was a lot of Mack Dawson in him, just as, unbelievably, there was a touch of Molly Stecker in her. "Oh, Michael," Gretchen said, shaking her head from side to side. She heaved herself away from the counter. "What am I going to do with you?"

He opened his arms to her. "Just love me," he replied, coaxing her with a husky tone to take the last few steps into his arms.

Gretchen took those steps, wrapped her arms around his neck, cradling his head against her breasts. "Michael Hamilton, you are really impossible," she murmured into the curls atop his head.

"Mmm," he agreed as he pulled her down on his lap. "That's what you probably love about me." His head descended, but before his mouth covered her eager lips, he hesitated. "You do love me, don't you?"

"I must," she whispered breathlessly.

That was all the encouragement Michael needed. He pressed her to him and kissed her with all the fierce impatience he had been trying so valiantly to control. Gretchen's senses reeled and there was only Michael, bringing her to life, demanding her passion. He tore his mouth from hers and showered kisses over her face, then caught her head between his large hands.

"We've got some weeks to make up for." He stood up with Gretchen in his arms and started striding toward the bedroom. "If you don't want to marry me, you're going to have to adopt me. I've quit my job in order to write fiction full-time. I hope you make a lot of money weaving or we'll both have to eat like birds until the royalties start."

"No problem, I've gone back to nursing. I think I can afford to throw a steak at you occasionally."

Michael smiled his approval. "Good for you, Partridge. I knew those strong nurturing instincts couldn't be stilled forever—look how you took care of me. I'm proud of you."

Inside the bedroom he used one foot to kick shut the door. "Now that I know you're a wealthy woman and can keep me in the manner to which I've become accustomed, I'm going to make love to you until you agree to marry me."

"What will you do after I agree?" Gretchen asked with a touch of impishness as she twirled the tip of one finger around his ear and pressed her lips into his neck.

Michael laid her gently down on her bed, then

shrugged out of his topcoat. "I haven't thought that far ahead." His topcoat hit the floor, immediately followed by his suit jacket, tie, and shirt. His fingers were at his belt buckle when he stopped long enough to growl, "Get out of those clothes, woman, or I'll rip them off of you."

"I don't know, Michael," she drawled tauntingly, but was already pulling off her boots. "I think you ought to do a little thinking ahead." Her boots hit the floor, then her socks and blouse. "A wedding does demand a little planning."

She shimmied out of her jeans and panties. She was reaching for the fastener of her bra by the time Michael joined her on the bed. With a single-minded determination that precluded conversation, he finished the job for her. His hands covered her breasts as soon as the wisp of lace and satin was gone. Having only one thing on his mind, his mouth swooped down to take hers in a kiss as powerful as the one they'd shared in the kitchen. His tongue drove rhythmically into the sweet moist velvet of her mouth.

He threatened with a rasping low voice against her damp lips, "I meant what I said. I'm going to make love to you until you agree to marry me."

Michael was so intent on making love to her, he hadn't even realized she'd agreed to his proposal. Gretchen couldn't help herself. She giggled out loud.

Michael blinked and froze above her. "That wasn't meant to be funny."

"It's not," she got out between bursts of laughter. "You weren't listening, but I've already agreed to marry you. Now what are you going to do?"

He uttered a loud expletive, then gave her a pleading smile that held an element of boyish disappointment—

but it was only the smile that was innocent and childlike. His body gave her more than ample proof of his maturity as he held her trapped between his legs.

"I was really looking forward to persuading you, Partridge."

With a triumphant grin, Gretchen teased, "I suppose I could retract my acceptance, but I've got a better idea, Dimple Cheeks. You see, unlike you, I've given this matter considerable thought."

She moved enticingly beneath him, running her hands along his hard flanks, then cupped his firm buttocks, fitting him closer. "We'll celebrate until sometime tomorrow." She arched closer to him. "I'm not using any caution, so you'd better be willing to legalize this union as soon as possible."

"Three days, Partridge. Just three days and then you're snared forever," Michael promised.

Gretchen knew there was no better fate for a little brown bird than this, but it was also a shared fate. Michael thought he'd cleverly captured her within his snare, but if he looked around he'd find himself in her nest. The meek partridge had successfully trapped the valiant hunter.

...now read on

Silhouette Special Editions. Longer, more involving stories of real love. And on November the 8th, Silhouette are publishing the Christmas gift pack of four brand new Special Edition romances for just £4.40.

Almost Heaven CAROLE HALSTON	**Tears in the Rain** PAMELA WALLACE
Remember the Dreams CHRISTINE FLYNN	**Water Dancer** JILLIAN BLAKE

COMING NEXT MONTH

MAN'S BEST FRIEND
Amanda York

Unshaven, uncombed and definitely untidy, Will O'Keefe had a face even a mother couldn't describe as handsome. But his charm and his appeal were undeniable, and despite her careful plans, Alex knew she had to follow her heart. Every dog has his day, and this was theirs.

ANGEL IN HIS ARMS
Suzanne Carey

Fate led Annie Duprez to Bourbon Street and into the arms of Jake St. Arnold. It was black magic from the first. Yet the past hung over them, an unanswered question with the power to force them apart. Did Annie have the strength to face the truth, even if it meant losing the man she loved?

LOVE LETTERS
Elaine Camp

The publicity for her first book was being handled by her old college buddy Whit Hayes, but Emmy felt differently about Whit now. If only he'd stop deluging her with roses!

Silhouette Desire

COMING NEXT MONTH

RED TAIL
Lindsay McKenna

Flying together gave them an intimacy soon strengthened by their growing need for each other when they were on the ground. Bram's passion unleashed her innermost needs, but Storm knew she was flying blind over dangerous waters.

FOOL'S GOLD
Beverly Bird

Clay didn't trust women without money. Devon knew he wouldn't believe it was his personality, not his bank balance, that drew her. And even if he did, there was another problem to deal with: the fact that she'd run out on him — fast — right after their first magical meeting.

THAT SPECIAL MAGIC
Laurien Blair

She loved health food, exercise, the outdoors. He loved pizza, beer and city living. When the two started fiercely protecting their own lifestyles, their love affair became a test of wills.

All it needed was...that special magic.

YOUR HEART'S DESIRE

Roses for
Remembering
ERIN ROSS

Hearts are Wild
GINA CAIMI

Bachelor Father
ANNETTE BROADRICK

A Glimpse of Heaven
LINDA TURNER

Silhouette bring you
your heart's desire this
Christmas. An attractive
gift pack containing four
brand new Desire
romances – sensual,
provocative stories,
written for today's
woman.

The Desire gift pack is
published on 8th
November at just £3.95.

Silhouette Desire Romances

TAKE 4
THRILLING SILHOUETTE
DESIRE ROMANCES
ABSOLUTELY FREE

Experience all the excitement, passion and pure joy of love. Discover fascinating stories brought to you by Silhouette's top selling authors. At last an opportunity for you to become a regular reader of Silhouette Desire. You can enjoy 6 superb new titles every month from Silhouette Reader Service, with a whole range of special benefits, a free monthly Newsletter packed with recipes, competitions and exclusive book offers. Plus information on the top Silhouette authors, a monthly guide to the stars and extra bargain offers.

An Introductory FREE GIFT for YOU.
Turn over the page for details.

As a special introduction we will send you FOUR
specially selected Silhouette Desire romances
— yours to keep FREE — when you complete
and return this coupon to us.

At the same time, because we believe that you will be so thrilled
with these novels, we will reserve a subscription to Silhouette
Reader Service for you. Every month you will receive 6 of the very
latest novels by leading romantic fiction authors, delivered direct to
your door.

Postage and packing is always completely
free. There is no obligation or commitment —
you can cancel your subscription at any time.

It's so easy. Send no money now. Simply fill in and post
the coupon today to:-

**SILHOUETTE READER SERVICE, FREEPOST,
P.O. Box 236 Croydon, SURREY CR9 9EL**

Please note: READERS IN SOUTH AFRICA to write to:-
Silhouette, Postbag X3010 Randburg 2125 S. Africa

- -

FREE BOOKS CERTIFICATE

**To: Silhouette Reader Service, FREEPOST, PO Box 236,
Croydon, Surrey CR9 9EL**

Please send me, Free and without obligation, four specially selected Silhouette Desire Romances and reserve a
Reader Service Subscription for me. If I decide to subscribe, I shall, from the beginning of the month following my
free parcel of books, receive six books each month for £5.94, post and packing free. If I decide not to subscribe I
shall write to you within 10 days. The free books are mine to keep in any case. I understand that I may cancel my
subscription at any time simply by writing to you. I am over 18 years of age.
Please write in BLOCK CAPITALS.

Name _____

Address _____

_____

_____ Postcode _____

SEND NO MONEY — TAKE NO RISKS
*Remember postcodes speed delivery. Offer applies in U.K. only
and is not valid to present subscribers. Silhouette reserve the right
to exercise discretion in granting membership. If price changes
are necessary you will be notified.*
Offer limited to one per household. Offer expires April 30th, 1986.

EP18SD